"JOE RANK "I'VE
COME T

A sudden silence gripped the Silver Queen. Rankin looked up and his eyes narrowed with a flash of recognition when he saw Dan Brant standing in the saloon doorway. Then his lips curled into a mocking sneer. People scrambled away from the bar, out of the line of fire, as Rankin's hand dipped to his pistol butt. But his gun's barrel was just clearing the holster when Dan fired his first shot. It jerked Rankin sideways and backward. The second shot tossed him into the orchestra stand, where he collapsed, bleeding mortally.

"Dan! Look out!" a voice shouted.

Dan wheeled and stared into the twin barrels of a sawed-off shotgun. He brought his pistol around, but his movement seemed agonizingly slow. He knew he was too late.

And then the roar of a six-gun blotted out his thoughts. . . .

BLOOD WAGER

WALT DENVER

ZEBRA BOOKS
KENSINGTON PUBLISHING CORP.

ZEBRA BOOKS

are published by

Kensington Publishing Corp.
475 Park Avenue South
New York, NY 10016

First printing: October, 1989

Printed in the United States of America

For Bill Letterman

Chapter One

The dead man swung slow in the wind.

From a distance he looked like something hanged in effigy, not human. Dan Brant knew different. The swirl in his gut told him far more than his steel-gray eyes. This was where the tracks had led him, this was what he knew he must find if he rode long enough, hard enough.

Dan's horse was weary. The rangy black gelding's sleek hide was streaked with sweat as if it had been draped in velvet streamers. The sun glistened off the ribbons of sweat. Flies boiled at the rivulets, trying to drink the salty blood that oozed from the gelding's pores.

Brant tugged the reins slightly as he rode under the cottonwood tree.

"Whoa up, Sugarfoot," Dan said, just to hear the sound of his voice in the awesome stillness. Not quite still; the rope with its deathly weight made the cottonwood limb groan, a sound that was as hideous as the twisted features of the dead man.

The corpse looked grotesque. The dead man's

neck was stretched beyond its normal length, the head crooked at an angle, lolling on the man's shoulder like a growth.

The hangman's knot was wound tight and thick, hugged the neck just below his left ear. The dead man's clothes hung in ripped shreds from his frame. Blood caked the trousers, the bare spots of skin. Flies clustered against the ugly purple wounds, gorging their hairy bottle-green bodies with the rust that had once been a man's blood.

The body was still warm, had not yet begun to bloat in the sun.

The stench of death cloyed the air. The slight breeze carried the scent over the plain, moved the smell up into the sky, where two dark birds stretched their pinions, floated on an invisible carousel. Dan looked up, saw the pair of buzzards circling, riding the currents with effortless grace. Their arcs tightened as they descended nearer the tree where the dead man swayed back and forth, his booted feet pointing to the ground, inches away.

Dan forced himself to look at the dead man again. He fought back the rising bile in his throat with an effort of sheer will, the burning in his guts and throat.

"Jesus, what they did to you," he muttered. It was a flat statement, not a question. He knew what they had done to the man.

The man had been dragged over rough ground before they strung him up. Dan choked on the thought of the suffering the dead man must have undergone, but he looked at the wounds. He wanted to remember them. He wanted to remember everything they had done to the man before they took his life.

The man's limp hands showed some of the torment he had gone through. They were scratched and bloodied, looked as fragile and bloodless as bone china in a blue light. There were rope burns on the wrists, as if he had been branded with a hot iron. His knees and the calves of his legs were torn by sharp rocks and stiff brush. His face was bruised, scraped raw over the high cheekbones, the mouth swollen and discolored from a battering that must have been brutal.

They did this, Dan knew, over a period of days. They made him suffer. They made his last moments of existence a living hell.

He looked at the man and saw his own face. A sudden chill froze the sweat on his flesh.

This could have been me, he thought.

The wind keened through the cottonwood leaves, the breeze picking up a sudden briskness, rattled the leaves against the branches. The sound was like the clatter of claws scuttling across a dark cave. The wind seemed to jar loose questions in his mind, questions that he must answer to assuage the grief and guilt that bobbed like corks in the dark sea of his brain.

Dan thought back a long way and tried to come up with answers.

The buzzards dipped lower in the sky, their wings like searching fingers in the blue emptiness. A quail piped in the distance, its voice sharp as crystal struck with a silversmith's hammer. A lizard on a liver-colored rock cocked its head, blinked a nerveless eye before gliding underneath into the shade.

Dan moved his horse closer to the dead man. He could no longer look at the faded, slack face, the broken neck.

Dan's eyes, smoky with anger, drew under their lids, flickering in cold hatred. He reached back for the skinning knife on his belt. He drew it from its leather scabbard, slowly urging Sugarfoot closer to the place where the dead man turned at the end of the hemp rope.

He placed an arm gently around the body, wincing as his hand touched the mortified hulk that danced so slow in the wind, a lifeless, mangled marionette.

Dan's other hand flashed upward and sawed at the rope. With a susurrant sound, like a scythe slicing through wheat, the fibers parted and he tightened his grip on the body. He rode away from the tree, the cut rope dangling empty, stripped of its prey.

Dan dismounted carefully, holding the stiffening body against him so it would not fall before he could support it on the ground. He laid the dead man down on his back, unable to look at his tragic countenance again.

He tied the reins to a chokecherry bush, then fished in his saddlebags for the iron tomahawk. He drew it out, its metal cold and brilliant in the sun.

It took him a long time to hack out a shallow grave. He laid the man in the chunk of earth he had hollowed out. He had to look at him again, then. He folded the dead man's arms across his belly, straightened him as best he could. He closed the lids over the empty, glazed eyes. Dan's jaw tightened as he took one last look. He stripped off his shirt and

10

covered the dead man's face. Something broke inside him and he choked back a sob. Tears stung his eyes and his throat ached, dry as day-old bread.

He scooped up the dirt he had dug and threw it over the body. His eyes seemed to cloud over with more steel, more gray, and behind them, a darkness that grew from flickering shadows. Dan forced himself to throw dirt over the dead man's covered face. He tried to be gentle, but an urgency was on him. He could no longer look at the frail remains of a once-alive man who was becoming part of the earth. Faster and faster he flung the dirt, listening to it spatter against parched flesh that was no longer vital, no longer capable of movements, words, a smile, or a simple handshake.

He took a long time gathering stones to pile up on the grave. The wolves and coyotes would not get to this body. The buzzards would not feed here. The buffalo would not pound over this place with slashing hooves. No wandering brave would take this man's scalp.

The wind died down and gentled to a breeze when the burial was over.

Dan wiped his sweat-soaked brow. He dug out another shirt from his saddlebags, slipped it on his sweat-slick frame. His clothes clung to his body, were stained dark from perspiration. His coppery hair was wet and fell tousled over his broad forehead.

He looked up at the sun. It was not yet noon. He took a swig from his canteen, then took his wide-brimmed hat off and poured water into it for his horse. The animal sloshed it down noisily while Dan rubbed its neck. The buckskin was fat and frisky, an Indian pony that had never tasted grain, could survive in country like this. He poured water over his horse's mane, shook out his hat, and put it back on his head.

Dan looked once more at the pile of rocks that was now a grave, then put the tomahawk back into his saddlebag. Its edges were dull and would have to be sharpened. He would do that tonight, when he made camp on the way to the lower fork on the Powder River. He mounted his pony and looked off to the west.

Without a command, the horse moved in that direction.

Dan didn't look back.

He looked at the path through the brush that led away from the hanging tree. The broken branches of chokecherry bushes marked a plain trail.

Three men had made that trail and he meant to follow it. Somebody had made a mistake—a big mistake. Somebody had killed the wrong man.

Dan knew they had taken the woman with them too. She had been with the man whose body twirled like a wooden puppet in the wind before Dan cut him down.

He thought of her, then.

He could see her blue eyes in his mind, smell the scent of her like crushed mint in spring, like honeysuckle and lilacs, sage wafting on an evening wind. He could hear the taffeta rustle of her skirts, hear her deep, full laughter flow over the prairie: bright and rippling, like a canyon full of brush afire, harmless enough but crackling loud.

12

His stomach tightened when he thought of her; thought of her pear-shaped face and her lips pursed red in a heart's contour.

The supply wagon was gone and so was Elaine Conroy, who had ridden with the man she loved, the man she had been planning to marry.

Dan reached unconsciously for the pistol at his hip. His hand tightened around the rosewood butt before he came back to the moment. There was no one here to draw his pistol on, no one to shoot, no one to kill.

He had killed before. That's why his jaw muscles tightened just then and he drew his hand away from the pistol butt. Some smoke, a lead ball flying into a man's flesh: these were things he had known before. He had thought it was all over. Now it came back, suddenly and without warning. A hand became a gun, a gun became death, the smoke became the spirit.

Who had told him that?

Gray Elk? Heraka Hinrota, his friend of the Sioux, had said something like that once. An Oglala, speaking from a long pipe, sitting on a buffalo robe in his tipi on the Powder. What had he said? Dan tried to remember.

"A gun speaks," Gray Elk had said, "and smoke is a river to a man's heart. The spirit is blown away with the lead ball, out of the mouth. The spirit is smoke, going high up. Into the sky. A man spits up smoke when he dies. It is his breath. It is his spirit."

His soul, Dan thought.

The Oglala were very wise. They thought about such things, but they were not afraid to die. They believed a man had lived a full life by the time he was twelve snows of age and every robe season a man lived after that was a gift from Wakan Tanka, the Great Spirit.

Dan shook these thoughts from his mind and thought of Elaine and her brother, Frank, who was waiting for him at the ranch near the Gallatin Valley.

The dream had begun to warp. A man was dead and a woman captured. The Powder, the Yellowstone, the Three Forks, all seemed very far away just then. Memories of the Sweetwater and the Little Bighorn, the great lush land teeming with game and gold, faded away as he came back to the present.

What was once a man had dangled from a tree, his spirit gone up to the sky like thin smoke. This man had breathed, had loved, had fought, had eaten the food from the earth that had now claimed him.

This man was now in a rough grave in an unknown place.

Dennis Brant lay in that grave back there, not yet thirty years old. It was a grave where he, Dan Brant, should have been. He was the one they were after.

They had just made a simple mistake. Anyone could have made it. Such mistakes had been made before. But, then, nobody had gotten hurt. This time a man had paid for that mistake with his life. A man named Dennis Brant.

Dennis Brant had been Dan's twin brother.

Chapter Two

Ed Rankin chewed on the twist and looked at his two sons riding ahead of him. Joe, the youngest, was the wild one, a lot like himself. Todd was more like his mother, but deadly nonetheless. There was a mean streak in Todd. He liked to watch a man squirm before he killed him. Joe liked to get it over with fast.

It was Todd's idea to hang Brant. Joe said to just shoot him and get it over with. Todd had dragged the man through the brush until he wasn't pretty to look at and then had watched him dance after he kicked his horse out from under him.

Joe hadn't liked it much. Too much waiting around. And when the girl had gotten hysterical, Joe rode off in anger. Ed had to slap her back to her senses while Todd just laughed like a drunken Cheyenne.

Ed knew there'd be trouble between the brothers over that girl. She sat in the wagon straight, like she was proud. Todd wouldn't be able to take that for long. He couldn't stand an uppity woman. Joe didn't even like women, didn't trust them. But there would be trouble, sure enough.

The woman was needed though. No more than a girl, she was the key to the Brant-Conroy spread up on the Gallatin.

"Hold up there, Joe, Todd," Ed ordered. "Time for some palaver."

The supply wagon came to a halt, driven by the only other man in the party, Larry Macabee, a man who wore his six-gun low on his hip and carried a short-barreled shotgun just in case he had to do close work. Larry had a scar on the top of his forehead where a Cheyenne had tried to take his scalp once. The scattergun had worked then and he swore by it ever since.

"What's up, Ed?" asked Todd, riding up. The girl in the wagon didn't lift her head. Her grief was still deep inside her, choking off her thoughts.

"Watch the girl, Larry. We want to talk private."

Macabee leered and said, "Take yore time, Ed."

Todd shot Macabee a look that was not exactly filled with kindness. Macabee sobered and the leer on his face withered away to a frown.

The three Rankins rode back down the trail out of earshot of the Conroy girl.

"Didn't want to say this back there," Ed said, "but I done think we killed the wrong man. That girl kept a-callin' him Dennis instead of Dan."

"I wondered about that," said Joe. He had light hair and hard blue eyes. He was lean from the saddle and short rations. His skin was tanned from wind and dust and sun, which made his blue eyes seem even brighter than they were. His older brother,

Todd, was darker, chunkier in build. But he had the same agate-blue eyes. All three men wore buckskins. Ed was taller and heavier than either of his sons. He was dark, with black eyes that were hard to see into, like marbles where the light never settles in one spot.

"If that weren't Dan Brant, he sure as hell was his twin," said Todd.

Ed gave him a long look. "I asked her what the feller's name was," he said.

"What'd she say?" asked Todd.

"Said his name was Dennis. Dennis Brant."

"He was a twin brother?" asked Joe.

"Maybe," said Ed. "Likely."

"You mean . . . ?" said Todd. "That guy was . . . aw, hell, I never heard of Dan Brant having no twin brother."

"Just the same," said Ed, "you took him awful easy."

"Yeah," said Joe, leaning over the pommel of his saddle. "He seemed pretty slow with his six-gun. I recollect seeing Dan Brant take out two men in Alder Gulch once't and they started first."

Todd reflected on this information as his father and brother stared at him. He worried the facts around in his mind like a chunk of tough meat.

"We figured he'd be the hardest of the two—Frank Conroy is just a cowpoke," said Joe. "Just a tag-along to Brant."

"They rode together," said Ed, "and Conroy stayed out of things."

"Yeah," put in Todd, "a kid scairt of his own shadow."

"No, we don't know that," Ed emphasized. "Conroy was there — if he was needed. He wears a pistol. Mayhap he knows how to use it too."

"I can outdraw his likes," Joe spat out. "A man don't mix it, he has his reasons."

Ed let that one send out its ripples.

"Brant picked his partner for a reason," Ed said a few seconds later, "and we know it isn't just because he's a fair hand with cattle. He might not need a backup man, fast as he is. I wouldn't bet that Conroy was a coward, though. Cool in the heat, sure. Our big problem now is that Dan Brant probably ain't dead."

"Them others sure run off quick enough," said Todd.

"Hired hands," said Joe.

The two boys worried the meat a little more. Both of them were chewing on Ed's words like pups not sure of whether they were getting fresh game or carrion.

"If the man we rubbed out wasn't Dan Brant, what's that do to our plans?" asked Todd.

Ed looked around at the country. Rolling hills had begun to appear like lumps in a flat bed. In the near distance the Black Hills rose up skyward, to the northeast of the Bozeman Trail. Soon, they would cross the Powder, the Little Bighorn, the Yellowstone, before reaching the Gallatin River to the west and the valley where the B Bar C lay. This was Sioux country, still, and called for careful riding. If they watched hard and didn't stumble on any hunting camps, they would be all right as they headed north. Ed didn't really expect any Sioux sign until after they crossed Crazy Woman Creek. It would be dangerous from there on, he knew, despite the presence of Fort Phil Kearney, which they'd have to skirt on their way through the Bighorns.

"We've left heavy tracks," said the elder Rankin. "He'll be on our trail for sure. Them others, too, don't forget about them. They got clean away, I'm thinkin'. If Dan Brant is on our behinds, he may have three others for company. The girl's our ticket to the B Bar C, but I didn't figure on fighting Conroy and Brant at once't. We mayhap got one ahind and one at the ranch. We need to do some figurin'."

Joe cocked his head and looked at his father.

"We could lay up and wait for Dan, if he is a-comin' on our trail," he said.

"He's too smart for that," said Ed. "He's like a wolf, that one."

"Hell, we could stay behind one of those hills yonder and pick him off," Todd snorted.

Ed laughed in derision. "Brant knows these hills too well," he said. "He's practically a Sioux hisself. Stayed with 'em four years or so."

He paused a moment to let his thoughts gather enough wool to say what he had on his mind. His raw, windburned face flamed with the ravages of weather. His sons waited for him to speak, their horses getting restless at standing too long.

"This girl's Conroy's kid sister, and as such she'll make a good bargaining chip for us once we get to the B Bar C. We got to beat them trail drovers we run off and keep Brant from catchin' up to us. Them thousand head at the ranch, along with these two hundred'll sell for plenty in Alder Gulch. Zeb Taggart will meet us at the Yellowstone with at least three other men. The B Bar C's just over the pass on the Gallatin River. We take the herd in, sell 'em in the gulch, and ride out with gold."

"That should be enough men to take care of Conroy," said Todd. "You sure Zeb will be there?"

"He'll be there," said Ed. "Conroy won't be expecting us. He'll see the herd and figure we're Brant's drovers. He ought to lay down his cards right there, I'm thinkin'. We can hole up there and take care of Brant and the others when they come up. If the Conroy girl is right, we got to expect him."

"He can catch us for sure, him with no herd to worry about," said Joe.

"Maybe we oughtn't to wait for Dan Brant to catch up with us," said Ed. "Reckon? Give him too much time to study what's a-waitin' for him and he'll be a caution. Joe, maybe you can help us out.

"You'll have to ride our backtrail after a while and bushwhack him," Ed told his son. "I figure he'll be in a hurry, maybe even by hisself."

"I can do it," said Joe.

"Sounds good, Ed," Todd said.

"Let's get to it, then, boys. We got a heap of ridin' to do." He turned his horse back toward the chuck wagon, where Macabee waited with the girl. His sons followed, sure that their father's plan would work.

When they rode up to the wagon they could see that Larry had been mauling the Conroy girl. She was backed up against the seat like a cornered animal, her eyes blazing with hatred and fear.

Ed flashed a hard look at Larry.

"We got no time for that," he said. "Rustling

cattle's one thing, foolin' with a woman what don't ask for it, another."

Macabee avoided Ed's gaze as he untied the reins from the whip post.

"Todd'll ride point. Joe, you take the left flank and I'll take the right. Let's get these cattle movin'. Larry, you bring up the rear. Make sure none of the herd lags back. We get to the gulch with these and the others, we can all be called mister."

Larry said nothing as he rattled the reins. Todd galloped ahead. Ed and Joe split up to take the herd's flanks. They rode over the tracks, mixing them all up before splitting off to the northwest to drive the herd up the Powder.

Elaine Conroy looked at the men's faces as they rode back and forth, keeping the cattle bunched. She shuddered inwardly, not willing to give them the satisfaction of knowing she was afraid. Ever since the murder, Dennis's brutal murder, she had known her own life was in jeopardy. She was determined, however, not to be brutalized in any fashion by these rough men who killed for pleasure, who plundered from better men because inside them was a weak core more animal than human.

"You think Taggart'd like her?" asked Larry when Ed rode up by the buckboard.

"Shut up, Larry!" Rankin snapped.

"Yeah, Zeb'd like her," said Joe.

"You, too, Joe. Keep your mouth to itself!"

The son ducked away from his father, his smile fading away to a dark frown.

* * *

21

The girl shivered in her seat, wondering what lay ahead now that she had heard such talk. Elaine wondered who Zeb was and why Ed Rankin had been so set on keeping his sons quiet. It was something to keep in the back of her mind. She knew that they were worried about Dan coming after them. She also knew that they had good cause for worry. Dennis had not been like Dan at all. Dennis had been a gentle man who usually let people take advantage of him. Dan was not that way. He was gentle, too, but he was firm in a way that most men weren't. He knew how rough the West was, and had become a part of it. His brother, Dennis, had been a follower. Dan was a leader. She had known them both a long time. Her brother, Frank, had grown up with them. Yet Frank was more like Dennis, a quieter, more tolerant man. He liked to work with the land, building things. That's why he and Dan had made a good team. Dan was a man who looked ahead and worked to make a living, backing his ideas up with a manliness that impressed her. Frank was a follower, too, but knew that men like Dan were needed to make a deal stick. The B Bar C had been their dream, a family dream, and they were all a part of it — or had been until these men had come along and killed Dennis.

Never had she seen such cruelty, such brutality. She had screamed so much, Macabee had had to gag her. But even so, she had seen the torture, seen the pain in Dennis's eyes as they dragged him over the rocks, bragging about how much better they were. But they had thought Dennis was Daniel, and she wondered then if they could have ever done such things to a man like Dan Brant. Would they have taken him so easily? Would he have let them do such a thing to his brother if he had been there? No, they would have had to kill him.

Right up until the end she thought they would let Dennis go. She thought they were just punishing him, teaching him a horrible, savage lesson. But when they put the rope around his neck, she knew they were going to kill him. Poor Dennis. He had looked at her so sadly, with such pain in his eyes. She could scarcely bear to face him, but she could not turn away from the pleading, the suffering, she saw in those soft gray eyes. When they slapped the rump of his horse, Dennis dropped two feet, until he took out all the slack. She heard a crack and saw his eyes snap shut. It was, finally, a merciful death despite the agony Dennis had undergone. But the bitterness remained in her heart, and the ache was like a knife through her chest. She felt terribly cheated before realizing that this was selfishness on her part. Dennis had been the one who had been cheated. Cheated of his life, of her love. Cheated of his future. Damn them! she said to herself. Damn them all to hell! And the tears flowed unbidden into her eyes and the ache swelled once again until she could scarcely breathe.

The buckboard moved out, Macabee cursing at the team. She watched Joe ride off to the west, Todd to the east around the herd as Ed drove the cattle ahead, toward the Powder.

The sky blazed with a rude sunset that marked the coming of night. Again Elaine Conroy shuddered, but the bucking of the wagon cloaked her fear for herself as she thought of Dennis again, reliving the agonizing days before he had been killed at the end of a rope.

Chapter Three

Dan Brant searched until he found the tracks of his three outriders, the men who had been with his brother Dennis. There would be no trouble picking up the trail of the stolen herd. Two hundred cattle cut a wide enough swath in prairie country. The chuck wagon would make the rustlers even easier to follow. It would take a hard rain to wash out the deep ruts. He wanted to make sure that Elaine had escaped. Maybe his men, Charlie Quinn, Wes Young, and Grady Sullivan had gotten her away when the trouble had started. His brother might have stayed behind to cover their escape, and so had paid the price.

His hands were riding toward the Crazy Woman. They had ridden fast at first and then slowed down. Their tracks told him that. They had obviously been fleeing for their lives. If Elaine was with them, all right. If not, then he would have to go after her captors. There were only three horses, however, and none of them seemed to be carrying any extra weight. A muscle in his lean face began to twitch as he felt the anger building in him.

He overtook the three men the next day. By their hangdog looks he knew they were not happy to see him. They had camped in a grove of cottonwoods by a dried-up streambed. There was no fire, no coffee on. They had left the scene of Dennis's tragedy without provisions.

Dan swung down from the saddle and looked at each of the men. Charlie, a flabby-fleshed man with a thickening beard, looked back at him with rheumy eyes. Wes, tall and lanky, looked down at his dusty boots and kicked at the dry earth. Grady Sullivan leaned against a cottonwood, a cynical look on his bitter face. They had been hired in Fort Laramie on the previous drive. Good men, but not fully set to the ways of the B Bar C. The spread was as new to Montana Territory as they were, so Dan could hardly blame them. He did want answers, though.

"I won't say anything," he said, "just now. Tell me what you can and we'll go on from there."

The morning had taken on a fuzzy, hazy cast, as if uncertain of its destiny. Dan looked at the sky and felt the earth warm up under his dust-caked boots. It was coming on to the month the Sioux called the Moon of Chokecherries Turning Black—August. He didn't know the exact date. It had been what the Oglala called the Moon When the Cherries Turn Red, July, when he had left Fort Laramie.

Wes was the first to speak.

"I guess we thought it was Indians, we bein' Colorado men and all. The Utes gave us some hard times back there until the settlers came. We were far out and the herd was a long ways away from the

26

wagon where Dennis and Miss Conroy was. There was a lot of dust and all." He finished awkwardly and there was a long silence while Dan looked at the other two men he had hired to drive his herd.

"Charlie?" he asked, looking into the bulky man's watery blue eyes.

"It was like Wes said. We was a long ways off and the herd was giving us trouble. These men came up shooting and hollering. Like they was waiting for us. They looked like a bunch of Injuns or raiders. We thought there was a bunch of them. They threw down on Dennis and roped him."

"Recognize who they were?" Dan asked quietly.

"We recognized them," said Grady Sullivan, his lip curling in contempt. "The same as what braced you back in Laramie. Zeb Taggart's boys."

Dan reflected on that for a moment.

"We thought Zeb had a bunch more there," offered Wes. "They were shooting their pistols off like it was a party."

"And you didn't help?"

The three men looked away from him.

"Hell, it was a terrible thing. The cows was wandering off and they had us dead and planted if we'd of rushed them. Miss Conroy was right in front of one of them. They had your brother roped around the shoulders. They saw us and was just waiting for us to come on."

Sullivan walked over to Dan and drew his pistol.

"We tried to fire at them, but half the caps didn't go off and the others were weak, so we knew we didn't have a chance. We had a rain the day before and our powder was still wet."

27

"How many were there?" Dan asked.

"We figured four. Four's what we could see," said Wes. "They had your brother. We thought they might let him go. There was no sense in stirring up more trouble than there was. If they just wanted the cattle, well then, why get killed over a few head?"

"Did you see what they did to Dennis?"

Wes and Grady turned their faces away from Dan Brant.

"We saw," said Sullivan. "We didn't want to look, but they made a lot of noise about it."

"What did they do?" asked Dan, his voice low.

"The kid dragged him a lot with his rope. I don't know what they did. They took out after us and we had to light a shuck. We figured the girl was safe if we made ourselves scarce. Dennis was done for. He was dragged pretty bad."

"You and Charlie agree with that?" Dan asked, directing his question to Wes.

"It was that way, Dan. We figured Zeb was around, waiting. Our guns misfired to beat hell."

"Keep them clean and oiled." Dan said. "They could mean your life or a friend's."

"Did—did your brother . . . ?" asked Charlie.

"They hung him," answered Dan. "Elaine is with them now, I reckon."

"Damn!" muttered Charlie.

"You want to go after them or light a shuck back to Colorado?" Dan looked at each of them, his face noncommittal.

"We're with you," said Wes. Sullivan and Quinn nodded.

"You ain't mad?" asked Wes.

28

"Let's get on their trail. Those cattle mean a lot to people up in Alder Gulch. They'll be needing beef this winter."

"How many are we after?" asked Grady Sullivan.

"Three, maybe four. Elaine Conroy is the problem. I figure we're four days behind them now. There are dozens of canyons along the Bozeman where they can hide a small herd like that. I'd like to catch them before they duck us."

"We're with you," said Charlie Quinn, his eyes clearing up.

"We've also got to warn Frank Conroy, my partner. If Zeb's in this, he'll go after the whole herd. Frank's got Lou Hardy with him at the ranch, and that's it."

"You know those men that jumped us?" asked Wes.

"The Rankins, I figure. The kid with the light hair is the one I wanted to drop back there in Laramie. I should have. A hothead. If there were four men, I don't know who the other might be. Zeb Taggart. Where is he right now? Maybe getting ready to take the herd at the B Bar C."

"They was the ones," said Quinn. "The old man seemed to be callin' the shots."

"Yeah, Ed Rankin," said Sullivan, "that's who it was." He shuddered as he said it and looked off in the direction of the Bozeman Trail as though making up his mind.

"We're awful hungry," said Charlie Quinn after a moment.

Dan walked over to Charlie first.

"Let's see your pistol and rifle," he said. He

turned to Wes and Grady. "Break yours out too," he told them. When he had finished his inspection, he stepped back. The guns had been cleaned and were loaded. He nodded his head in satisfaction.

"We'll shoot a rabbit or two along the way," said Dan, going for his horse. "Let's try and make it to the Crazy Woman before dark."

The four men mounted their horses and rode west, back to the Bozeman Trail. Ahead of the others, Dan searched for the tracks of the cattle along the route. It was just before dark when he cut the sign of a lone rider west of the trail. He dismounted and studied the track for a long time while the three cowhands fidgeted in their saddles. Hunched over, he took a close look. He stood up, glad there had been light enough left to see. In an hour the sun would be over the Bighorns to the west and it would be dark.

"We'll cross the Crazy Woman in a while," said Dan, climbing back up on his mount. "Let's get to it. Fan out and see if you can't scare up a couple of rabbits for supper."

Charlie made a face. "We had that for lunch," he said.

"Well, it's not likely we'll find any beef along here. Now, if you want to ride up close to the Black Hills and try for buffalo," Dan said, "then go right ahead."

Charlie shook his head and spurred his horse while drawing his pistol.

Dan kept his eyes moving, glancing over both sides of the trail looking for an ambush spot. He wasn't looking for rabbits. There had been no cattle tracks, only the lone horseman's. A shod horse carrying weight, moving slow. It would be one of the Rankins, but which one? The light-haired hothead? The dark-haired brother? The old man? They'd take the herd up the Crazy Woman, skirt the fort, and probably cross the upper fork of the Powder. A thousand places to hide two hundred head up there. A thousand places to ambush a man. Four men.

The tracks were at least three days old. There was probably no reason to worry. But that wasn't what made Dan ride west of the trail. He was looking for the other tracks, to find the pattern. He disappeared from view of the others and kept moving in the direction of Tensleep.

Ten minutes later he found what he was looking for. The herd had passed that way, the wagon too. He found another set of hoofprints belonging to a lone horse. He kept riding west. Another horseman on the left flank. There was the pattern. The wagon and one other man were driving the herd. The two flankers were lagging behind, probably crisscrossing every few miles. Dan felt the hackles rise on the back of his neck.

They were expecting him to follow!

He rode back to the Bozeman at an easy gallop. The herd had to follow the water, but he didn't. He thought he could figure out where he could head them off. It wouldn't be on the Powder, but either at the Tongue, the Rosebud, or the Little Bighorn. They could cut back into the Bozeman Trail at any of those points, but he'd bet money it would be between the Rosebud and the Little Bighorn. The beginnings of a plan began to form in his mind.

He heard shots and figured the boys had a rabbit or two on the run. More shots a little later. Then, a single shot. "Well, they got at least one," he said aloud to himself.

They camped at a glade near Crazy Woman Creek. The creek made a lazy, gurgling sound. It was low from the summer heat, but Dan knew the water was clean and cool. It was a good enough camp, better than some. Too near the water, maybe. Water made noise and you couldn't hear a man sneak up on you in the dark. The Utes, he knew, never camped near a stream or a river. Instead, they pitched their lodges on high flat ground, where they could see any approaching enemy for miles. They hauled their water, but they were brave fighting men, their women hardworking.

Charlie had two rabbits skewered on wood spits over a fire dugout. The meat crackled and dripped on the fire. Charlie, always the hungry one, did the cooking while the others munched on berries they had found growing in the thickets, berries the Sioux had missed that summer.

"See any more sign?" Wes asked Dan while they were eating the rabbits.

"They're heading up the creek to the north fork of the Powder," Dan replied. Before this was over, he'd have to tell them, he knew. They would figure it out soon enough for themselves. He'd wait, though. One of them would bring it up. These men were slow, maybe, but they weren't stupid. They could add and subtract. But until he had driven those cattle to their destination, he had thought it best to keep certain facts to himself. Some men were downright peculiar toward Indians. Some couldn't see beyond the war paint to the man inside.

"Where they goin'?" asked Charlie.

"My guess is they're heading for the B Bar C to get the herd there. Hook up with Zeb Taggart somewhere between the Yellowstone and the Gallatin."

"Around Bozeman Pass?" offered Sullivan.

"Maybe. I think the Rankins have realized their mistake. If they didn't figure it out for themselves, Elaine Conroy told them about Dennis and me. They're watching their backtrail and I think they're hoping to get another crack at me."

"What're we going to do?" asked Charlie nervously.

"They've got cattle to slow them down, so we cut the time from three days to two days already. That's how far we're probably behind them. We leave early in the morning, don't stop at Kearny, and we gain a day, maybe two."

Dan got a stick and began to draw in the dirt next to the fire. He drew the Bozeman Trail, the rivers ahead.

"Here's where I figure they'll come back to the trail." He drew an X between the Rosebud and the Little Bighorn. "I'll be waiting for them."

"What about us?" asked Charlie, the practical coward. "We plumb got the williwaws over this chunk."

"Boys, let's forget about what happened back there with Dennis. You got jumped for fair and didn't know how to get out of it. I bear you no grudges. But Frank's going to need you at the B Bar C. He'll need the information you're going to give

33

him along with your pistols beside him. Lou Hardy's the only man there right now. They don't expect trouble. Far as Frank knows, Zeb's still in Colorado. I don't know what he's doing out here, but I picked up talk back in Laramie. He's been cutting some kind of a swath out here. Some of the talk said he was hooked up with Pete Langly up at Gold Creek and Virginia City. Bad bunch."

"Yeah, I heard of them," said Charlie.

"Well, you've got to get to Frank and warn him. Zeb may be on the Gallatin now, in fact. He may be watching the ranch, waiting for Rankin to show up. Be careful when you ride up."

"We will," said Wes Young.

Grady Sullivan looked at Dan.

"I can't figure out why we were driving two hundred head in when there were over six hundred bought back in Laramie besides them," he said.

"All right," said Dan. "You boys deserve an answer to that. You may not like it, but if you think about it, it makes good sense in this country. We've got a thousand head or so at the B Bar C. Those miners at Alder Gulch and Virginia City near starved to death last year. We'll drive that beef in there just before snowfall and sell it on the hoof. The two hundred head were never going to the B Bar C, nor to the Gulch."

"They weren't?" asked Sullivan. "Then where was they goin'?"

"Up the Rosebud to where it meets the Yellowstone."

"Why you said they were headed that way now. I don't get it," said Wes.

"That's why I won't need you boys. Those cattle are a present for my friend Heraka Hinrota, Gray Elk. He and his band are camped up thataways. The buffalo have been shot out on their hunting grounds and I'd like to see them raise beef. Their sun is setting awful fast, and I think Gray Elk knows it."

"Damn!" muttered Charlie. "We been driving a herd of cattle for the Injuns!"

"Maybe that's why you're still wearing your own hair," said Dan quietly.

Chapter Four

The men mulled over their thoughts in silence. Several moments passed before one of them spoke up.

"That's right, Brant," said Wes Young. "You lived with these Oglalleys for a time."

"About four years," Dan admitted. "But they're getting restless. The gold brought too many white men on to their hunting grounds. They can see their land being eaten up by men who don't care about the earth. They hold it mighty dear."

"Aw, hell, if they can't hang on to it, they don't deserve it," said Sullivan.

Dan stood up and tossed the stick into the fire. A muscle rippled in his lean cheek. He took a deep breath.

There was no changing these men's minds. Like many who came westward, they had heard stories of red-men atrocities, maybe had gone through some bad experiences with Indians themselves. There were good and bad of both races, but the prime problem as Dan saw it was that the white man thought of the

Indians as pests, as intruders on land they wanted for themselves. They could not understand that the Indians were hostile toward the whites because they, too, claimed the land. Not only the land, but their way of life. While it was often a brutal life, at bottom it was very simple and honest. The white man had made himself into an enemy many years before. The Indian had been willing to make friends, but many of the red men did not understand either the ownership of land or the white man's greed for the gold and silver in that land. Nor could the red man understand the white man's need for lumber and minerals such as lead and zinc. To the Indian, these were things that belonged to the earth, not to human beings.

The question would not be resolved at this campfire nor in council. The Indians were not part of the grand scheme. They stood in the way of progress and so they had to be eliminated. The only chance for survival of the red races was if the Indian adapted to the white man's ways, blended into white society, or at least lived in peace on its fringes. These were questions, and answers, that Dan Brant had studied for a long time. They had first started surfacing when he lived among the Oglala, learned the way they lived, the way they thought. Such ways of living and thinking were in direct contrast to his own upbringing. He doubted that many men wrestled with their consciences over such matters as he had. It was a damned shame, but it was something he'd have to live with, just as Gray Elk would have to live with it.

"We'll get started early," Dan said. "We'll go together as far as the Rosebud. Then you ride hard for the ranch and tell Frank to hold on until I get there."

"All right, boss," said Wes.

"I'll take the first watch. You can toss a wet rock to see who's next." Dan walked upstream a ways and found himself a spot where he would make no silhouette in the moonlight. The voices of the men carried to him for a time and then faded away.

He was attuned to such surroundings. The solitude had been a part of his life for a long while now. The Oglala had taught him much. His friend, Gray Elk, had taught him the Sioux beliefs and they had seemed sensible, more sensible than most of the white man's. The Indians believed that all things were alive, even the stones of the earth. They respected nature and did little tampering with it. They would never uproot a tree and always apologized for taking poles down for their lodges and travois. They thanked the game they killed and knew of the endless cycle of life in all its forms. They knew that nothing could be taken away without penalty. Whatever was taken must be replaced someday. The grass that the antelope and the buffalo ate was composted by their own tribe's bodies. All of the creatures of the earth were their brothers — except the inexorable white man. It was a tragedy being played out, Dan knew, and the Indian, whose land this was, stood alone and surrounded at the center of it.

His reverie was broken by the sound of a rifle crack. Instinctively, Dan ducked and slid into the shadows behind a tree. He drew his revolver and crouched. He tried to discern where the shot had come from, but in the darkness he couldn't be sure.

38

The scent of black powder wafted to his nostrils and he knew that the shooter had been close, perhaps less than fifty yards away, upwind.

He listened. It would be hard for a man to move on such a still night and not make any sound. A hunter, Dan knew that the ears were often better than the eyes for discovering the presence of game. The moonlight splashed the night shapes of nature with silver. It was eerie, quiet, the kind of quiet that roars in a man's head like the wind in a seashell. Dan strained his ears to hear what he must hear. But he didn't move. He didn't make a sound.

Something then. Something moving. A soft rustle, not far away. Dan stifled his breath, moved his head almost imperceptibly. The sound came from a different direction. It was a cautious sound, like that of a man sliding a boot or a moccasin onto a stone.

Whoever he was, he was good. Dan felt a twinge of admiration. Not many white men could move that quietly.

But where were the others?

Asleep, maybe, before the shot, but surely not now. A deaf man could have heard that shot, could have felt its vibrations. Something, someone, must have gotten to them, slipped into camp, put a knife in each one. Three men! It was hard to believe, but there was nothing stirring yonder. The moon seemed to stir up whispers as it moved silently over the broken landscape. Dan had to move. He needed to know where his adversary was, who he was.

He kept low and moved in the direction where he had last heard sound. He thumbed his pistol's hammer back, squeezing the trigger slightly so that the cocking mechanism made no sound as the sear was engaged. He fingered the cap; it was tight on the nipple. The Remington .44 was heavy in his hand. He wished he had his rifle, but the .44 would be enough gun if the range were right. It also had the advantage of giving him five extra shots without reloading. He slithered across a rock like a lizard, scarcely making a sound. Something told him to keep moving, to get behind another tree, fast.

Dan moved. There was no way to do it without making noise.

From his right, and above him, another shot rang out. The ball crackled as it ripped through bark, then whined as it sang off a rock, beyond. This time Dan saw the fire from the barrel, the spew of sparks from the burning black powder. He fired once, the pistol bucking in his hand. He fired again, lower and to his left. Then he fired to the right, covering. He heard a thunk on the second shot and a muffled cry of pain. The air was foul with the taint of burned powder. He listened for the sound of a powder horn or flash, the copper spout clacking against the barrel. He listened for the whispering sound of a ramrod pushing patch and ball down over the powder.

He heard none of these sounds. But a moment later he heard brush cracking underfoot, what sounded like a groan, and then a body moving rapidly away, kicking rocks loose, tearing at branches.

Three shots left in the pistol.

He decided against trying to reload in the dark. The three full cylinders would have to do. Dan rose up from his cramped position and started after the sounds. He came to the spot where he had shot at he ambusher. He peered at the rock, the ground. He wiped at a spot on a large stone near his feet. His finger came back wet. He tasted it. Blood. Salty. He wished it were daylight so he could look at the true color of it. A man could tell, sometimes, where his ball had hit by the color and texture of the blood.

So, his man was hurt and he was trying to get away. It was dangerous to track a wounded armed man at night, yet it might be possible to overtake him before he had a chance to reload his rifle. He probably carried a six-gun. Most men in the territories did, for one reason or another. Mainly for protection or reassurance, the latter being a dangerous reason in some situations.

Dan followed the sound in his tracking. The moonlight played tricks with his eyes. Still, he was able to see some sign of the man's passing: a broken branch, a dark wet splash on the side of a tree, making him think the wound was low, in the leg, possibly in the side.

There was no way he could be sure, of course, but instinct and experience told him that his man was not fatally wounded. Instinct told him that even now the man might be waiting for him in a pocket of land, behind a tree, in a draw, his hammer cocked. Dan slowed down, moved more cautiously, continued to listen intently. He still held his pistol in hand, at the ready. He kept track of the direction he had traveled so he wouldn't become lost in the dark.

A thrashing noise some distance ahead of him caused him to pause, to sort out the sound in his mind. There was silence, then the unmistakable creak of leather. A moment later he heard the crack click of shod hooves over stone, the rustle of horse flesh under leather moving away from him, heavy in the night with its muscular weight, its breathing.

"Damn!" Dan muttered under his breath.

He raced ahead, hoping for a clear shot. He broke into a meadowy clearing. At the far edge of it he saw the horse and rider. The rider was leaning to one side, his right, favoring the left. Dan brought his pistol up straight ahead of his eyes. He sighted down the barrel and tried to calculate the range, the lead, all in an instant. He cocked the single-action Remington and, holding low across the horse's rump, moving his hand to the left for the lead, squeezed off a shot. Flame shot from the barrel of his revolver. Horse and rider disappeared in the trees.

He couldn't tell for sure if he had hit the man. Objects were tricky at night. The distance was uncertain. Soon he heard nothing more. He stayed in the shadows at the edge of the glade and caught his breath. The grasses were silver-gray and silent. After a while he moved to his left, in the direction of camp. He would track that man in the morning.

When he came to a safe place where the moonlight was bright enough, Dan stopped to reload his pistol. He emptied the charge into the empty cylinder, placed a round ball atop the cylinder, and rammed it home, brushing off the thin sliver of metal that remained from the oversized ball. He pulled a tin of bear grease from his pocket and smeared it in all of the cylinders, since the previous blasts had burned most of it away. He wiped his pistol and holstered it. Then he made his way slowly back to camp, careful in the way he walked.

The three bedrolls were still, eerie in the wash of moonlight. Dan circled the camp to make sure that the man he'd hit hadn't doubled back on him. Satisfied, finally, that there wasn't another ambush waiting for him, the tall man crept up to one of the bedrolls. The rheumy eyes of Charlie Quinn stared up at him, glazed over with the film of death, glistening oddly in the moonlight. In Charlie's neck someone had cut a wide smile through the flesh, severing the larynx. Charlie's mouth was open, as if he had tried to cry out. Dan drew a blanket over the head and moved quickly to the next sleeping bag.

Grady Sullivan was dead, too, his throat savagely cut. He lay on his stomach. He had tried to crawl away, it appeared, and the loss of blood had stilled his movements. A large pool of it was spread out where he had breathed his last.

Dan heard a moan.

He raced to Wes Young's bedroll. He threw off the blanket.

"Dan," Wes croaked. The assassin's knife had missed his throat. Instead, there was a deep gash just below it, in the top of the chest. Dan lifted Wes in his arms. The wound in his chest wouldn't have killed him. The bones had held the knife back, kept it from penetrating deeper in its hasty slash.

"Stomach," Wes managed through tight teeth.

Dan ran his hand down to the cowhand's stomach. It came away sticky with blood.

"Who was it, Wes?"

"One of 'em. Slipped up on me. Gawd, it hurts."

"Yeah. Was it Ed Rankin? One of his sons?"

43

"Son. Joe, I think."

"Take it easy. Don't try to talk anymore."

Dan thought fast. Yes, it would have been Joe. Folks said he was mean for the sake of being mean. He fancied the knife, too, and he wouldn't bother to give a man a chance. Yes, Joe would pick this way to kill a man. Sneak up on him in the dark and cut his throat. Laugh about it later.

He dragged the bodies of Charlie and Grady over to a shallow ditch, blankets and all. When he got back, Wes was dead too. He dragged him into the makeshift grave and began piling stones over the bodies. It was the best he could do.

When he was finished, he moved his own camp deeper into the woods, under a deadfall, where he couldn't be seen. He turned the horses loose and tied his own where it could graze some on the already drying grasses. In the morning he would begin to hunt a man.

As Dan bedded down, he heard the far-off howl of a wolf, its keening cry chilling the August night. He could sense the changing of the seasons. Soon it would be the time the Sioux called the Moon of Drying Grass, September. He heard a deer snort near the creek. The Indians would be coming back from hunting Pte, the buffalo, about now, tanning the winter hides, making the robes and blankets, curing the meat. Heraka Hinrota would be wintering along the Yellowstone in another month, hunting deer and elk for the last of the meat before the snows locked them in until spring.

Somewhere out there was a killer, Joe Rankin. He had made Dennis suffer, had carved up three good men with a Bowie. Dan had to find him before he could track his father and brother. They would come later. Joe was like an animal gone bad, killing for the sake of killing. Dan could not rest until he'd culled him from the herd of good men. When he found him, he would kill him without mercy, the way he would kill any predator.

These thoughts gave Dan no satisfaction. It was a weighty thing to kill a man. It was weightier still to kill a man in cold blood. But that was the way he felt. Dennis murdered brutally, three good men cut to ribbons as they slept. Such actions demanded equally brutal reactions. Joe Rankin had given up his own right to live. Live by the sword, die by the sword.

Dan slept lightly, attuned to the night sounds. Once, his horse nickered, but grew quiet again, grazed on the remnants of summer grasses. An owl floated by on silent wings, hunting. The moon drifted off through the trees and left blackness in its wake. A rabbit screamed in the grip of sharp talons. And then it was still, until morning.

Dan was up before dawn slashed a peach-colored rent in the eastern sky. He saddled his horse and checked his guns and powder. He built no fire, nor did he linger. He rode off, chewing on a chunk of jerky. Within a half an hour he had picked up the trail of Joe Rankin. It was difficult to follow. He found where the man had bedded down, tended to his wound or wounds. The earth had been dug up, leaves scattered. Some of the leaves were bloody. The

45

man hadn't built a fire to cauterize his wound. Perhaps, Dan thought, he was not hurt so bad after all Or, he could have poured black powder into the wound, ignited it with a sulphur match. There would be no need to heat a blade, touch it to the flesh, had he sealed the wound that way.

Excited now, Dan spurred Sugarfoot, following the tracks of the outlaw's horse northwesterly across a grassland tinged with salmon, burnished with a ruddy gold. The buckskin, sated from grazing all night, seemed eager and fresh. Soon the horse broke into a lope. Dan sat the saddle, rocking easily to the animal's rhythm. The hills, sere and tawny at the twilight of summer, seemed gentle. Dan was not fooled. Somewhere ahead there was danger. Joe Rankin would be hurting. And Joe would be watching his own backtrail like wounded prey.

This was, thought Dan, a hard land, with hard men in it. Rankin would be waiting for Dan to catch up to him. The trail was easy to follow now. Rankin had made no attempt to conceal his passage.

And why should he?

Rankin had the advantage. He knew where he was going. Dan could only follow, blindly.

Except Dan Brant was not blind. And he was no fool.

Chapter Five

Joe Rankin knew he had to keep moving. He had to find his father and brother, get them to back him. He had no illusions about Dan Brant. Not anymore. One of Brant's bullets had streaked through his left leg, tearing flesh and cartilage, bruising the bone. He had had to stop and pack dirt and leaves in the two wounds. Luckily, the ball had passed clean through. It had left an ugly channel. The exit wound was nigh to .60 caliber, he figured.

The jolting in the saddle jarred his wound. Shoots of pain burned through his leg until, after a while, it went numb. He needed to wash the wound with alcohol or water. He was sure the lead would poison him if he didn't. Yet, he rode away from the Powder, hoping he could reach his father and Todd up on the Tongue, dress his wound there. He would have to move faster than he was, but every step of his horse brought searing pain to his leg. He would have to stick to the Bozeman Trail and skirt Fort Phil Kearny. There would be too many questions he couldn't answer, too many things to account for if he was to stay there to wait for Brant to catch up to him.

The Bozeman was a dangerous road, especially in 1866, despite the three forts that had been put up that year. Some called it the Bozeman Trail now, but it was also called the Bozeman Cutoff and the Montana Road. It was a shortcut to the gold fields, cutting out some 400 bone-tiring miles. The gold-hungry travelers with their overloaded wagons no longer had to cross the Continental Divide twice to get to Alder Gulch, Virginia City, and the other rich diggings around the Tobacco Root Mountains, along the Grasshopper River at Bannack City.

The Sioux hated the Bozeman Trail and they attacked the wagon trains often. A lone traveler had more chance of survival than a group. In fact, John Bozeman and his partner, John Jacobs, had marked the trail in 1863, finding it easier to stand off Sioux than to fight the high peaks of the Rockies.

Joe knew it was his only chance. Cattle were slow-moving animals. They had to graze as they traveled. The beef had to be in good shape, in even better shape at their destination, and Ed knew that. Two hundred head were as hard to handle as a thousand in that country. Ed would be drifting them off the trail often to avoid trouble with the Indians and any challenge by an army patrol.

Joe kept up the grueling pace despite his pain. He angled toward the Tongue River, where he felt sure he would rendezvous with his father and Todd. If not, there was plenty of wild country along the river, up the canyon where it emerged from the mountains. Lion and elk country, broken, ragged, with numerous small canyons, plenty of cover in case he had to lie in wait for Brant. Behind him, he knew, was a man he had missed, a man bent on vengeance. The thought spurred him on, and after a time he began to watch his backtrail and to pick places where his trail could be lost by a tracker.

He stopped at the top of every hill and looked back over his shoulder for at least five minutes. His eyes scanned every inch of the backtrail, searching for any slight movement, any change of shadow or light. In country like this a man could be invisible if he was still. Especially at long ranges. Dan Brant would be a man like that. Hard to spot in the brush, impossible to see among the junipers, the cedars. But if he kicked up dust, if he rode across a far hill, Joe would see him. He was wary, but he kept moving on, driving himself beyond his pain, goading his horse through hard country that taxed lung and leg to their limits. The pain returned, however, and the terrible weariness. But he knew that Brant would come. If not today, then tomorrow. If not tomorrow, then the next day. He would come.

This is what saved him, for a time. Half crazy with agonizing pain, he became clever in his delirium. He picked his way through even rougher country; followed creek beds, doubled back over hard ground, and took another course. Eventually he made his way to the Tongue and then rode down it, into a clump of cottonwoods and aspen and stunted juniper, to a point where it met the bloody Bozeman Trail.

And there he waited, his .45-caliber Berdan rifle loaded, his six-gun loose in his holster.

* * *

Ed Rankin couldn't understand it. Two bunches of Sioux had come upon them and had not attacked. One bunch had even cut out some cows, arrogantly, then returned them to the herd after checking out the B Bar C brand. It didn't make sense. He and Todd had been ready to draw their rifles from their saddle scabbards, but the Indians had ridden away both times.

"Whatcha think them redskins wanted?" Todd asked his father.

"I don't know. My scalp felt awful itchy there for a spell."

"No foolin'. Well, some of 'em hankers to play games like that. We better keep our eyes peeled from here on in."

"I don't like it none. It ain't natural."

"I bet Macabee's constipation went away that last time." There had been eight Sioux in the party. Six of them had rifles which they kept trained on Todd, Ed, and Larry Macabee while the other two, expert horsemen, cut several cows out of the herd. Then, mysteriously, they had run the cattle back in, and with wild whoops had ridden away over a hill. Their cries lingered in the still afternoon air.

"Bring Larry and the girl on up. We'll camp at the next stream, get an early start in the mornin'." Ed started pushing the herd ahead of him. They were sluggish and he wanted to reach the Tongue by noon. He was worried about Joe. He should have made his loop by now. Six days they had been pushing the herd.

50

Ed had been boiling inside for a long time. Now that Joe hadn't shown and the Sioux were acting up, his nerves were on edge. He kept touching the butt of his .44 Colt of 1851 vintage, rubbing the wood grips as if for reassurance.

He was angry because Zeb Taggart hadn't told him everything. Zeb had just held out the carrot and he had followed blindly like a goddamned donkey. Oh, he could guess at some of it. It was more than the cattle, he knew. They were part of it. Not just these two hundred head, either. The thousand or more head at the B Bar C were to be stolen and driven in to Last Chance Gulch or somewhere. He knew that much. But the plan was too daring to be just that and no more. Zeb had something else up his sleeve. This was almost like suicide, driving cattle through this country. Might as well have a marching band and carry banners emblazoned with FREE CATTLE in big block letters. The Sioux had a taste for beef same as a white man. And, with buffler bein' so scarce, they sure as hell weren't picky.

It wasn't only the Sioux. The Cheyenne and Arapaho also hunted here. Ever since Bozeman had opened his road, the redskins had been swarming like smoked hornets because the game kept getting scarcer and scarcer. No, Zeb had some big thing in mind, and he was determined to pull it off, quick and brutal, then light a shuck out of the territory. There were vigilantes now, and the army. Soon there would be bona fide lawmen with sawed-off Greeners, or some capable of tricky pistol work gunning down the lawless men who preyed on the settlers and gold seekers.

51

The trouble was, Ed didn't know the whole picture, and that rankled him. He didn't like to be kept in the dark. It was plumb crazy driving cattle through Sioux and Cheyenne country. What in hell was the man up to? Well, too late to fret on it now. He had been dumb enough to jump when Zeb snapped his fingers. But, Ed thought ruefully, he should have asked a lot of questions before taking on this job. A lot of questions.

"Larry, set out ahead and get the camp set up at the next stream!" Ed roared as the chuck wagon came alongside.

"Yeah, Ed," said the man, whipping his team. Elaine Conroy shot a dark glance in Rankin's direction before the wagon jolted her away.

"Come on, Todd, let's keep 'em movin'!" Ed shouted to his son. "We're two hands short and a long ways from supper!"

Somehow, the two men managed to do the work of four without spooking the herd. They were sweaty, gritty, and mad when they saw the cattle stream out, finally, and head for water. Larry had the chuck wagon set up on a grassy knoll, under shade, no more than thirty paces from the creek. Todd and Ed sat their horses while the cattle drank, then moved them out to grazing space and bunched them up. They hobbled their horses and let stringers trail from their bridles.

They ate smoky beans and stringy antelope that was just a touch above spoiling. Antelope was poor man's meat in such country. But there were plenty of them and they were easy to kill. A man could lie on his back and stick his legs up in the air, work them

52

like scissors and the pronghorns would come up close to take a look. They were curious and stupid, but they could run like the wind. There was grumbling, naturally. They had two hundred head of beef and were eating shoe leather. Larry had heaped in some extra fat to kill the taste and to give them all some gumption for the next day's drive. The beans weren't quite done. The coffee was bitter from not-quite-cured beans, but they drank it anyway because there was a chill to the night and the brew was warm.

Ed looked at Elaine Conroy, wondering why she didn't complain about the food. Maybe she was one of those spoiled eastern women who couldn't cook and didn't know the difference. In fact, she hadn't said a word in the past three days. He had tried to give her some privacy, but she was, after all, a prisoner. He let her sleep under the wagon and made Larry throw his blanket some distance away. He didn't want anything to happen to her before he delivered her to Zeb.

"It won't be long now, miss," he told her. "You'll get to see that brother of your'n."

Elaine's eyebrows rose slightly.

"Well, you want to see him, don't you?"

Elaine shrugged.

"You got a tongue, woman?" Ed snapped.

"I know you mean to harm my brother. I've seen the way you and your sons take pleasure in cruelty. My brother is not a violent man, nor would I wish it so. But I sincerely hope, Mr. Rankin, that he shoots you and your sons dead."

Her voice was an icicle on the air, needling every man there. Todd gagged on his coffee. Larry's eyes

53

glittered in the firelight. Ed's jaw hardened.

Inwardly, Elaine was pleased. Her words had had the desired effect. For days she had built up to this moment. She wanted the men edgy, off balance. Todd got up, as she knew he would, to take the first watch.

"Guess I'll get out to the herd," he told his father. "Can't do no good here."

"See you at midnight, son," Ed said as he had said for the previous five nights.

"Guess I'll get 'er done," Larry said, rising to his feet, also predictably.

Elaine watched Todd walk out to the herd, carrying his rifle. The herd was located over a rise and couldn't be seen from their camp on the knoll. Their sound, however, carried to the fireside. Elaine waited, wondering if she had the courage to do what she must do. Underneath her long dress she wore riding breeches. The pockets were stuffed with tidbits of food, scraps that she had hoarded ever since that first nightmarish night when she had learned that her brother was the next target of these outlaws.

She was counting on the men doing the same things tonight that they had done on previous nights. They were, she discovered, like most people, creatures of habit. She was counting on their sticking to routine, and, so far, they had not varied one whit from their schedule on previous nights. Yet, she was apprehensive, and careful, because she knew the kind of men surrounding her. If she made a mistake, their guns would speak first. She was unarmed, and would die, like Dennis.

Elaine was determined not to make a mistake. She

nurtured her cup of scalding coffee, careful to keep it from cooling. She watched the fire, kept Ed in her sight, listened to Larry banging his pots. She knew just where Larry hung his pistol. Every night. In the same place. She judged the distance from her spot by the fire to where the gun belt hung. She calculated the distance from the chuck wagon to the horses.

It might be that she would have to kill Larry Macabee. Or Ed Rankin. She kept herself from shuddering. She had never shot at a man before. She had killed, but only for food. Her father, Richard Conroy, had taught her and Frank to shoot, to hunt. She was a good shot with pistol or rifle, could ride with the best of them. She didn't mind the messiness of black powder. She had cast balls and made a special grease for patching. Her mother, Wanda, had never had a mind for such stuff. She died young of consumption, her husband following her to the grave a few years later. So she had hunted with Frank and made do, and she knew she would have to summon up all her skills now. To survive.

She wondered if she had the courage to kill a man. Up close. The thought was abhorrent to her. But she had seen what these men had done to Dennis, and her anger was so deep, she thought she could kill Ed and his sons. Maybe. Maybe if she thought about it too much, she couldn't. But if she thought of Dennis . . .

The beans were still sitting by the fire on a stone. Steam curled upward from the iron pot, indicating that they were still hot. Elaine watched the tendrils of vapor spiral upward in the air, her eyes glittering as excitement fingered her nerves. She felt the tingle of something in her veins, the excitement of getting ready for a shot at a buck or a rabbit. She looked over at Ed and saw that he was bringing out his makings. She had counted on his doing that too. He always had a smoke after his evening meal, seldom at other times. Tobacco was too precious to use all the time, especially when a man was a long way from a town.

She shot a glance at Larry. His gun belt still hung on the wagon. It seemed to be the biggest thing in the universe at that moment. He was scooping up dirt in a small bucket to use to clean the pots and pans. He would get some ashes, she knew, to mix with water. She must act soon, before he came back to the fire. Both men were dangerous. She had to act fast and sure. She looked back at Ed. He was pouring the tobacco out of his leather pouch into a paper held in his hand. He was totally absorbed in this action.

Elaine wet her lips with her tongue. Her throat was very dry. She longed for a drink of water. She looked quickly at the horses. She knew she would have to be very fast.

She reached down for the bean pot. She felt its warmth even before she touched it. Macabee started toward the fire, carrying an empty can in his hands for the ashes.

It was time!

Elaine grabbed the hot bean pot and scooped it through the fire. She flung the hot coals in one swift motion straight at Ed Rankin. She stood up in the same motion as the man cried out in pain and confusion, his hands tearing at his burned eyes. His screams sent a spurt of sensation along her backbone, made the hackles on the back of her neck rise. She turned, hurled the bean pot at Larry, then ran for the wagon. She grabbed the gun belt off its hook and drew the loaded pistol.

She raced for the nearest bridled horse, her heart in her throat. Behind her she heard the chilling cry. "Stop there, girl, or die!"

Chapter Six

Dan thought he had it figured out. There was no use wasting any more time tracking close. For some time now, he had been switching back and forth, picking up a scrambled track. Joe was trying to throw him off, but a running man couldn't put back every overturned stone. He couldn't ride on rock forever. Fact was, Dan knew Joe was headed somewhere. And the only sure landmarks in this open, unclaimed land were the rivers and streams. There were no blazes, no trails beyond what the buffalo made, no stone cairns to mark a man's way. If Joe was going anywhere, he was going toward the Tongue. A tracker had to use his instincts, play his hunches. A man could follow a sign only so long as it was consistent. Or he could use his head and think like the hunted one. Dan did that now. He knew the country. He knew where a man would have to go if he was wounded and didn't want to stay close to forts or settlements.

He had picked up enough of Joe's tracks to know where he was most likely headed. The question was, would Joe meet up with his party or would he be alone? The cattle would need graze and water. The Tongue was a likely place and the timing would be about right. The Bozeman made good use of the creeks and rivers that abounded in the region. He knew he would have to be careful, though. Joe could be waiting for him at any spot along the way. Still, his best bet was to ride for the place where the Tongue met up with the Bozeman. He could circle until he cut sign or saw his quarry. He spoke to his horse and checked his rifle and pistol again.

Dan's main concerns were Elaine and Frank. If Zeb was behind all this, all their lives were in danger. And there was good reason to believe that Zeb was back in the picture. They had crossed paths before, back in Cherry Creek, which the people were now calling Denver. Dan had been there like many another man, but not after the grains of gold that snuggled in the Plattes or the St. Vrains, or Cherry Creek itself. He had, as always, been a cattleman, a provider of food for the hard-pressed pioneers of the western regions.

Zeb had rustled then, but no one could prove it — until Dan came along and exposed him. Zeb and his bunch had been driving cattle in with three or four legally registered brands, all of them designed to blot or run on other legitimate brands.

It was more or less an accident that Dan had found out the truth of Zeb's operation. The accidental part concerned a sick cow. The nonaccidental aspect of Dan's discovery came about because he had a hunch and played it through to its conclusion. On any other day he might have passed up the opportunity, but he'd had trouble with Zeb's herd and drovers. They had continually chopped up the good grazing spots and let their herd drift into his, cutting out some of his cattle when they retrieved their own. It was enough to get his suspicions up.

Dan remembered the day he had made an enemy of Zeb Taggart. The events had crossed his mind several times since then. They were in his mind now as he rode after another of Zeb's men.

There had been an urgency to get to Cherry Creek and the diggings there, he recalled. Zeb's bunch had pressed ahead on the last stretch, leaving some of their cattle in bad shape.

"Frank, let's take a look at that dying cow from Zeb's herd," Dan had said, riding off on a tangent from the rear wing of his own herd.

They rode over to the cow. Its tongue was lolling from its mouth, swollen, purple. Its eyes were glazed, its breath shallow. Dan drew his .44 and put the dying animal out of its misery with a shot to the brain.

"I want to check that brand close," Dan said. He and Frank dismounted.

"It's a Double B, one of Zeb Taggart's," Frank said.

"Yeah, on this side it is."

Dan drew his bowie knife and took off the patch of hide that carried the brand on the left hip. He scraped the fat off and held it up.

"No Double B there, Frank."

"Well, I'll be . . . the Double I brand!"

"Zeb's right handy with a blotter. Let's just take this into trail's end and see what this man Taggart has to say about it."

"That'd be trouble, Dan. I've heard he's a hard man." Frank was not one to push trouble. That's what Dan liked about him. He liked to think things out first, carefully. Dan was the same way. The habit had kept him alive.

"I've known Chester Ivers for nearly ten years," Dan said. "He's had a hard time with rustlers. I figure he's got a stake in Zeb's drive. I aim to see he gets the proceeds from the stuff that's his. A man who'd use a running iron needs to be taken down a notch or two."

Frank looked at his partner and nodded. He felt the same way. The inner scars of the hide showed plainly what had happened. Someone had taken a reverse 3 and burned it into each I, making the brand a Double B, one of Zeb Taggart's, duly registered. Ivers's spread on the Brazos was fairly well known. If Dan called Zeb, there'd be trouble all up and down the trail. Chester had been losing cattle for quite a spell. Texans were proud men, and they had long memories.

In Cherry Creek, Dan sought out the foreman of the Taggart herd at the stockyards, below Larimer Street. This was a man named Bernard Butler, the source of the Double B brand. Dan made sure there was a crowd around as he pulled the cowhide out of his saddlebag.

"You left a dead critter a day out," Dan said coldly, unfolding the hide for all to see. "A skinning shows you blotted the brand."

There was a deathly stillness in the air. The stockyard foreman came up to Dan and grabbed the hide

61

out of his hands. He turned it over. Twice. Other stockmen came over and examined the telltale piece of cowhide. The buyers grouped around the bunch and viewed the damning evidence. Dan kept his eyes on Butler.

"That's a Double I," Dan said, "underneath. Chester Ivers's brand."

"You coulda run the brand yoreself," Butler said coldly. "That don't prove nothin'."

"Cut another out, Butler," Dan said. "I'll pay for the cow. We'll skin it out."

Butler lost his composure for an instant. Men's eyes turned toward him. He let his right hand drift toward his gun belt. He stood some distance from the milling men, in the open. He looked up at Dan, who was astride his horse. Dan didn't move a muscle. His eyes bored into Butler's.

"These cattle are bought," said a man named Willie Letterman. "I'm willing to drop once since everyone knows that Brant's cattle will bring less money on the market now that Zeb's herd beat 'em in. Ralph, cut out a Double B and slaughter it. Cut out the brand."

A cowhand jumped off the fence and two more men followed him. They split a Double B cow out of the herd. Ralph slit its throat and bled it. He made a cut along its backbone and a semicircle around the hip brand. He scraped off the fat and blood, exposing the inner lining of the hide. He carried it over to the huddle of men and placed it alongside the hide that Dan had brought in. There was a ripple of muttering voices.

"Another Double I underneath!" someone exclaimed.

That's when Butler went for his pistol. His reach was fast, but his hand seemed to move in slow motion when Dan's own hand blurred to his holster, came up full and bucking. Butler's barrel hadn't even cleared his holster when the first ball caught him just above his belt buckle. A look of angry surprise spread over his face as the second ball brought a small puff of dust just off center of his breastbone, hammering a furrow straight into his heart.

Another Taggart cowhand started for his pistol. Dan leveled his barrel at him.

"Two can be read over just as easy as one," he told the nervous man. The other's hand stopped moving. The man shook his head and stepped back.

"By damn, where's Taggart?" Letterman shouted angrily.

"Over to the Double Eagle most likely," someone replied.

"A minute, Letterman," Dan said, his voice booming. The crowd quieted. "Have you paid Taggart off?"

"I was just on my way to give him a draft now," Willie replied.

"Check the brands real close. One draft should go to Chester Ivers's account."

"I'll do that, Brant."

"Now, who gets top dollar for the rest of these cattle?" Dan asked coolly. It was a bold move, but Dan knew he had the upper hand. He could push a little, while everyone was off balance. No use in letting Taggart get the whole hog when he had already been proven a rustler.

"Zeb Taggart's a cow thief!" a man shouted.

Letterman whispered to the other cattle buyers. Dan kept his pistol in plain sight as he looked over the men around the corrals.

"You'll get top dollar for your herd, Brant," Letterman announced. "Taggart's got some questions to answer."

Satisfied, Dan rode up to Larimer Street, where the Double Eagle was located, and tied his horse to the hitching rail. Word of what had happened at the stockyards preceded him. Taggart had gone, not out of cowardice, as Dan learned, but because he had thought his cattle deal concluded. Zeb Taggart had ridden out an hour before.

Dan had not heard of Taggart since, nor seen him. Dan had never avoided Taggart, whom he knew on sight, but their paths had not crossed since that drive to Denver.

Until now. Dan was certain that the big man had bided his time and was now trying to exact his revenge. He grew more and more sure that Taggart had engineered the death of his brother, the theft of his cattle. He knew that the Rankins were in cahoots with Zeb. Taggart was shrewd. He would use men like these for his own ends. He was sorry that he hadn't followed his trail back in Cherry Creek so long ago. None of this might have happened.

The tall man picked his way carefully along the Tongue, skirting the thick willows, threading his way through mountain alder and birch, leaving behind the aspen, spruce, and fir as he neared the Bozeman. The thick trees gave way to open places, where grew the yellow rose, puffed clematis, and antelope bush, the signs of autumn already on the land, the grasses seared to a pale sienna, the leaves of the quakies turning a brilliant yellow-gold among the evergreens.

He drifted off into shadows, following obscure game trails, stopping often, listening. He flushed a herd of bedded muledeer once, watched a raucous trio of crows taunt a red-tailed hunting hawk. No man tracks caught his eye, and the Bighorn mountains in the distance seemed to draw nearer. He watched beaver building a dam, oblivious to his presence. When he rode on, he heard the slap of a paddle tail. He jerked in the saddle and smiled. It had sounded like a gunshot.

This was grand country, and he could see why the various Indian tribes loved it so. It must have been magnificent before the white men came, with plenty of game and fish, endless acres of unspoiled land. It was magnificent still, with the jagged Bighorn horizon, soft blue mountains rising above a shadowed land that teemed with life. There was a pulse to the land, a heartbeat. He felt it surge and thrum in his temples, stir deep emotions that he had come to recognize and acknowledge during his years with the Sioux. Here a man could find all that he had ever wanted or dreamed of, could he live in peace with his neighbors, could he but roam free and take his sustenance from the land, only from the land.

Closer to the Bozeman, he began moving in a zigzag pattern, ranging across a wide swath, looking for sign. If Joe Rankin was hoping to meet up with his bunch of scoundrels, he wouldn't bother being too careful so close to his destination. Dan knew he would probably stay east of the Tongue since he, too, would be looking hard for sign now—sign of the stolen herd.

If he followed the Tongue up into the mountains, however, he would have a better chance of getting away. The woods were thick there, the mountains formidable. A man could hole up there for a long time and not be discovered if he was smart. If he made no fire and he hunted with the snare or the deadfall, he could survive for some time. It was something to think about. Dan had a hunch, though, that Joe Rankin didn't want to go to high ground this late in the summer. The Rockies had their own weather, and it seldom paid attention to the seasons on the flatlands.

Dan found what he was looking for on one of his swings across a faint game trail that led to the river.

The tracks were fresh, no more than two hours old. Moisture beaded up in the hoof marks near the stream. They were easy to follow. Dan swung wide, trusting to his hearing and vision now. The Bozeman was not far off. He sniffed the air, hoping to pick up the scent of trail dust or the cattle. Instead, he smelled smoke.

Would Joe Rankin make a fire?

It was possible. The man's wound might be bad enough by now that he'd have to cauterize it. Or, if he already had, maybe the jolting in the saddle had opened up the wound again. In this country, a man had to take care of such things himself. Dan edged into the trees and moved with a ghostly slowness. The aroma of smoke was elusive. He wet his finger and tested the faint breeze blowing in his direction. Even as he did this, the breeze shifted slightly. He looked up at the sky. Clouds were building up on the horizon. The breeze shifted again, coming up behind him. No doubt, he reasoned, there would be a storm that night or by morning if the wind picked up. It was circling now like a sniffing wolf, a sure sign that they were in for some heavy weather before long.

He had to pick his way very carefully now. He avoided the brush and rock, keeping to the soft, dying grasses underfoot. The smoke smell grew stronger. The horse seemed to sense the change in its rider. It stepped softly, its ears perked, rubbery nostrils distended, quivering at every vagrant waft of smoke. Dan whispered to it soothingly. He patted its neck and spoke low in the Oglala tongue, baby talk, about its being a *shunka chistala*, a little dog, a *shunka witko*, a wild dog, and *tashunka hunkacila*, a horse boy.

Soon Dan spoke no more, not even in whispers. He ranged to a high place and looked over the country, at the patches of glistening river he saw through the trees, the Tongue. He looked for smoke, not really expecting to see any, since his quarry no doubt would have built his fire where the smoke would be dispersed through the trees. Yet it could be that Joe wanted the smoke to be seen, by his father and his brother. Or as a trap for Dan himself.

Dan sat his horse, still, for a long time before he spotted the faint wisps of smoke curling up into the darkening sky. He had to squint to make it out, a gray variation in the sky above the trees near where the Tongue narrowed next to the Bozeman Trail. He estimated the distance. Less than a half mile. He worked his way up a gentle rolling hillock to a higher level, closer. The smoke now hung there in a thin gossamer pall as the breeze died down momentarily. He could no longer smell it.

He circled, climbing still more. Finally, he had a view of the trail in both directions. He looked off to the northwest and the clouds had moved across that section of the sky. He looked to the southwest and saw a telltale cloud of dust in the direction of Fort Phil Kearny. It wasn't much, only a different shade of sky, but it was enough. He started down, in the direction of the smoke on the Tongue.

When he was close enough, he stopped, got off his horse, and tied the animal to a tree. He slid his rifle free of its buckskin scabbard and checked the cap. He worked his pistol in its holster. It slid back and forth easily. He took off his boots and pulled moccasins out of his saddlebag. He changed his footgear and put the boots in the bag. He crouched low, and began moving toward the smoke like a stillhunter, stopping every few feet, changing direction, avoiding the dead branches that would make noise if they snapped. It took him the better part of an hour to travel the quarter mile that remained.

He was no more than a susurrant shadow through the trees. He crept to a knoll, where he could lie low and see in three directions ahead of him. He slipped over the edge of the knoll and looked down toward the river. His lungs filled with air as he saw the small fire, the man lying next to it holding a knife next to his leg. Dan could almost smell the burning flesh. Joe winced with pain, but made no sound.

Dan brought his rifle up to his shoulder and scooted quietly toward a thick cottonwood tree to use as a backbrace. He wiped the sights of the .50-caliber Hawken, made for him in St. Louis by one of the gunsmiths in Samuel Hawken's shop, not many years before. He sighted down the barrel and drew a deep breath.

He cocked the hammer back, squeezing gently on the front trigger. The lock made a small clicking sound. He pulled the second trigger, setting the first trigger up to respond to the slightest touch. He waited to see if Joe Rankin had heard either of the tiny clicks. He curled his finger around the front trigger and was about to squeeze when he saw Joe throw his knife aside and struggle to rise. That's when Dan heard the pounding hoofbeats of a horse. His head jerked to the left and he saw Elaine Conroy racing in his direction.

"Dan!" she yelled.

Time seemed to stop still at that instant.

Dan rose and swung his rifle back to Joe. That's when he saw it was too late. He brought the barrel down even as he saw a flash of orange flame and a puff of smoke from Joe's pistol. He squeezed off a shot from the Hawken just as he felt a sledgehammer whack into his shoulder and twist him around. All of the air whistled out of his lungs in a rush.

A sickening wave of nausea swarmed up from his belly. Dan saw the sky twirl over his head as he rocked back against the tree behind him. He was dimly conscious of reaching for his pistol, drawing it, and firing in Joe's direction. Joe was a thin, scrambling stick moving away from him through a glazed and watery pane. Still, he felt the pistol buck in his hands, again and again.

69

He heard a sharp cry from somewhere nearby and then he fell forward into blackness.

Chapter Seven

Elaine Conroy screamed as she watched Dan Brant fall face forward to the ground. It happened so fast, she didn't know where the shot had come from. It was all so unexpected. One moment she was desperately hailing a friend, the next, Dan was pitching to the ground as if he'd been felled with a sixteen-pound maul.

Terror gripped her. Panic seized her senses. Her throat constricted and her scream died in her lungs.

She reached Dan just as she saw Joe Rankin limp to his horse and climb on. She picked up Dan's pistol and shot twice at the young man before he disappeared from view. She knew she had missed. Breathless, she sank down beside Dan and lifted his head up into her lap.

"Dan, Dan, it's me, Elaine!" she pleaded.

Her arm was drenched with blood. Quickly, she turned Dan over and, with her teeth, ripped free the hem of her dress. She tore off a strip and wrapped a tourniquet above the slashed groove of his wound. She found a stick and placed it in the cloth, tied the

71

material around the wood, and twisted it to staunch the flow of blood.

She knew he was in shock. He had hit his head severely when he fell. She tore another strip of cloth from her dress, ran to the stream, dampened it, and returned. She heard the man moan and knew that he was coming around.

"Dan, can you hear me?"

"Yeah, I, uh . . ." he groaned.

"We've got to get out of here."

Dan's eyes opened. He saw Elaine's face swimming above him. He sat up, the sky overhead distorted, swirling like roiled waters. Just looking at the sky made him dizzy. He felt overcome with nausea. She helped him to his feet.

"Where's your horse?" she asked.

He pointed with his right hand. Elaine reached down and handed him his pistol. He holstered it.

"Joe Rankin?" he asked.

"Gone. But the others will be here soon. Can you ride?"

"I'll have to." He looked at his arm. The blood flow was slowing down. He felt dizzy and disoriented, but he knew he could make it.

"Get your horse, Elaine. Follow me."

He checked his pistol. There was only one ball left. Like many other men of his day, he carried spare pistols, slung on the saddle horn and in the saddlebags. When he reached his horse, he exchanged his nearly empty one for a fully loaded Colt's Army. He put the Remington into his saddlebag. Gingerly, he climbed into his saddle. He almost fainted again, but held on until the swimming feeling of dizziness passed. Elaine rode up, her eyes anxiously looking into his.

"We've got to get to your brother, warn him," Dan said. "Let's head up the Bozeman. I'll be all right."

She nodded, her face white with concern. She looked back at the cloud of dust to their rear. Dan noticed her movement.

"They might have heard the shots, but I doubt it. Joe will join them, that's for sure. Ed might send Todd after us, or come himself. We've no time to waste."

"How close do you figure?" he asked.

"I got away only a short time ago. Close," she said.

Dan grimaced. The pain struck him then, full force. It made him sick all over. He fought against sinking into unconsciousness again. If he went down now, he figured, he'd stay down. Elaine was not strong enough to get him back on his horse. And there was no time. They either rode out of danger now, or they faced two or three guns, maybe four.

He knew he would have to attend to his wound soon, pack it with cool mud and leaves. It was beginning to swell and throb, but that was better than the hard jolt he had felt before. He had lost a lot of blood, but, thanks to Elaine's quick thinking, not enough to be dangerous. His greatest worry was infection. He had a bottle of whiskey wrapped in a small cloth bundle inside one of his saddlebags. That would have to do to wash the wound.

Looking at her out of the corner of his eye, he could see that she was exhausted. Probably scared to death too. Her face was pale, wan from the strain of the twin ordeals. He knew she must have gone through something to have escaped, but he did not ask how she had done it. There would be time for that when they were able to stop for the night. But first he had to put distance between them and their pursuers. He felt sure they could make the Rosebud and then they would begin to climb, to head west for the pass. Just beyond was the B Bar C, and Frank, Lou Hardy, a couple of other hands, perhaps a drifter or two. Mountain men were always stopping by for a meal or for talk. Sometimes one or two would stay on, help out, just to get the feel of civilization back in their bones before they faced real towns and people not used to their rough ways.

At one point Dan stopped at a high rise and looked back. Far off he saw a speck that might have been a rider.

"Are they following us?" Elaine asked.

"Could be. They would be going too slow now, I'm thinking. There's a storm coming."

Elaine looked at the sky. The clouds were scudding in over the Bighorns. The wind picked up as if to emphasize Dan's statement.

"Where did those come from?" she asked. "Rain?"

"Anything. The mountains make their own weather. I'd say snow."

"Snow? In August?" She shivered. "We must take care of your wound."

"Summers can get short out here," he said dryly. "We'll camp on the Rosebud, a place I know there. It's not far. The weather will blot out our backtrail."

Dan stepped up his horse's gait after that. They would need shelter and warmth. Elaine, he knew, was already cold. It would get colder. As they neared the Rosebud, he wondered who was following them, Todd or Ed Rankin himself?

He'd bet it was Todd. Ed would stay in reserve, or wait until he joined up with Zeb. He was the fox. Smart and canny.

Dan's assessment of his pursuers was right on the mark. When Elaine escaped, she put a serious kink in Ed Rankin's plans.

Ed had been angry that the Conroy girl hadn't stopped when Todd had shouted at her. He cursed his son for not having shot her, winged her at least.

"You're soft, Todd. Damn your hide. She would have shot you, given the chance."

"I don't hold to shootin' no girls, Pa. I figured to run her to ground sooner or later."

"She's a spunky one. Lot of grit. You'll run a long way 'fore you corner her again. Zeb'll have all our hides for this."

"I reckon," Todd said. They had herded the cattle in silence until, nearing the Tongue, they stopped up short at the sound of gunfire. Puzzled, they jerked their rifles from their saddle scabbards, sat in wait. When Joe came riding up, Todd gave a shout.

"It's Joe, Pa. He's back!"

"Packin' lead, it looks like."

Joe slid from his saddle as his father and brother rushed up to him with questions.

"I killed Dan Brant," Joe panted.

"You sure?" asked his father.

"Pretty sure. He come up on me back there on the

Tongue. The girl too. She caught both of us off guard, but I spit some lead at Brant and he went down like a stone."

Ed's eyes widened. He looked intently at his son. "What about the girl? Where is she?"

"She picked up Brant's pistol and started in a-shootin'. Come pretty close too. I lit a shuck. Why'd you let her loose?"

"We didn't let her loose," Ed said sarcastically. "She got away. You should have gotten her."

"She may still be there, Pa. I got me a wound's openin' up again. It's mighty sore."

"Larry!" Ed called. "Tend to Joe's leg here. Todd, you find out where the shootin' was. Get that girl back. If'n Brant ain't dead, finish him off. Don't come back until you do those two things."

"Sure, Pa," Todd answered. "What're you gonna do?"

"We're due to meet Zeb on the Yellowstone, this side of the pass. I'm leavin' Larry with the herd to make his own time. I can send men back to help him with the drive. That girl may know the country. If so, she's got to go through the pass. We'll be awaitin' for her or for both of 'em."

"What if I get her first?" Todd asked.

"Then Zeb won't be so danged mad at us. We'll go on to the B Bar C as planned. I'll see Zeb in no more'n two sleeps. You be there in three sleeps, no later. Now, get crackin'."

Joe looked at his father, a question in his eyes.

"Come on, Joe, we'll see to your wound. Larry's got stuff in the wagon can ease your misery."

Todd took along some grub from the chuck wagon

and rode off while Ed looked at the bullet wound in Joe's leg. Larry Macabee searched through the wagon for salves, medicants, and bandages.

" 'Pears you cauterized it right well, son," Ed said. "Clean enough hole. Should heal up in no time. Chew on a bullet and let it scab over. You'll be fit in no time."

"I'm gonna kill Dan Brant," Joe said.

"If'n your brother don't get to him first. Brant's a handful."

"I almost got him, Ed. I shoulda got him. Maybe I did."

Ed turned away from his son in disgust.

"Hell, Joe, you ain't makin' sense. Babble, that's all it is. A man ain't dead until you see the buzzards at him," he growled.

Macabee leaned out of the wagon, his arms laden with cans, bottles, gauze, and cotton. Ed looked at him with contempt. "Put that stuff away. Warn't nothin'. Keep it dry and clean, it'll mend all right."

Larry dropped the stuff in a heap and climbed down to the ground. "You two'll have to handle the herd from here on in, Joe," Ed said. "You work with Larry, hear? I want every head to cross that pass. Keep 'em movin'. Let 'em feed, but don't let 'em slack up too much after you cross the Little Bighorn. You got a long stretch from there to the Yellowstone. I'll likely see ya at the B Bar C. Watch yore hair."

"Yes, sir, Ed," Macabee said. "We'll be there directly."

Joe was sullen. He didn't like being left behind. He was hurting bad. The ball had gone through his leg, but he thought it must have bruised the bone. Luckily, the lead hadn't torn an artery, or he'd be dead now. Still, the wound throbbed and he hated the thought of driving cattle through a storm over the pass. They would have to move slow, and if Brant took a notion to come after him, he'd be a sitting duck. It would do no good to argue with his father, though. He knew that. Once his old man had made up his mind, that was that. So Joe just sulked and watched as his father made preparations to leave them behind.

Ed filled his saddlebags with provisions and rode off without another word.

"The son of a bitch didn't even say good-bye," said Joe bitterly.

"Well, now, Joe," said Larry Macabee, "that ain't no way to talk about your pa."

"Shut up," said Joe.

"Well, I'm glad he ain't my old man."

"You just shut up, Larry. I ain't in no mood for your mouth. We got a long ways to go and a hard drive to get there."

Travel on the Bozeman was light, almost nonexistent at that time of year. There were serious considerations by the government, the army, to close the road because of the extreme danger it presented to travelers. This was a fact that Zeb Taggart and his bunch had taken into consideration. But even so, some would use the cutoff because it saved time, never mind the dangers. Ed Rankin was one of those. He rode into the teeth of the gathering storm, heading for Bozeman Pass and his rendezvous with Zeb. He knew the country well and skirted the usual routes, cutting down the distance he would have to travel.

Taggart's plan would have worked, he thought wryly, if Dan Brant had been killed. Instead, they had lost the hostage, that damned stubborn girl, and that was another mistake.

Ed knew that it would be best to see Taggart and explain matters to him alone. Otherwise, his sons' lives might not be worth much. Zeb had an obsession about Dan Brant ever since that day at Cherry Creek. It wasn't only the money he had lost, it was the fact that another man had bested him. That the man was also in the right made the loss doubly hard to take. Zeb had wanted Brant dead and he'd wanted him to die slow. Maybe, though, there was a way to convince Zeb that the mistake was even better for him. Brant would hurt a while longer, grieving for his twin brother.

He was hoping that such an explanation would calm Zeb down, make him see that he would still get his revenge. After all, Dan Brant wasn't no better'n the next man. Tough, maybe, but so was Zeb Taggart, and Ed had no doubt about his own abilities with a gun. Brant couldn't, by God, live forever. He was just lucky, that was all.

Ed hadn't reckoned on the fierceness of the storm. He thought, in fact, that it might blow over, dump some rain and then clear up. But that was not the case. One moment it was calm, the wind waiting with bated breath. The next, the wind rose with a shuddering velocity, cutting at him like a fresh-stropped razor. He turned away from the wind, heading back to the safer path, the Bozeman Trail. Snowflakes began to sift in from the north, blowing like loose feathers on the fierce gusts.

Rankin pulled up the collar of his coat and fished gloves from his saddlebags. The snow thickened and the wind subsided. The flakes grew larger and a calm settled on the trail. The temperature dropped and the snow began to stick to the ground. He was in the open, and his eyes sought shelter through the curtain of drifting flakes. Soon, he knew, the trail would be wiped out. He would lose his bearings long before the light faded.

Still, he rode on, wanting to get as much distance as he could before he had to stop and make shelter. He hoped to strike the Rosebud or the Little Bighorn before dark, before the snow got too thick to ride over. If the wind came up again . . .

The snow began to fall faster and faster. Visibility dropped to a hundred yards, then fifty, to twenty-five. He could still make out the wagon ruts of the trail, signs of settlers moving through the territory to the gold fields, but his eyes burned from the strain. The landscape was even more desolate now that the snow was locking it in, confining his vision to a scant few yards ahead and on either side.

There was an eerie silence settling about him as he rode. The sound of his horse's hooves were strangely muffled. The wind came up again and the snow began to blow at his back, extending his vision. Flakes stuck to his sheepskin coat, to his gloves, to the space between his horse's ears, to its mane. He brushed them from his eyelashes, shook them off his hat like flour dust.

Soon he could hear only the sound of his own breathing and his horse's. His breath spumed from his mouth in steamy puffs as the temperature continued to drop. The light from the sun shrank away in the west and he used it as a guide to keep himself on the trail as he remembered it. An hour of light, more or less, was left to him. He had lost his sense of distance once the storm had closed in about him. He might be close to the Rosebud, might be drifting away from it toward the Little Bighorn. He kept angling toward the sunglow, the pale light to the west.

The trail was still defined, and trackless. He wondered where Todd was. He should have been ahead of him, leaving tracks. Or, maybe he had taken shelter before the snowstorm had hit. Ed's senses sharpened in the void of the falling snow. He slowed his horse down and listened until his ears hurt. His eyes burned from the whiteness surrounding him. His horse bent its head and snorted, began to fight the bit.

"Not yet, you bastard," Ed muttered, digging his spurs into its flanks. "Got to get to the water."

The trail widened and Ed stepped up the pace. The Rosebud couldn't be far off.

"Pretty soon, boy," he said to the gelding. His breath was smoke, his heart pounding. He hoped he was right. A man had no business being alone in such country at such a time. The trail was littered with the bones of men who had been caught out in weather. Winter never let on when it was coming. It showed no mercy when it did come.

The light in the west seemed to falter, then surge

to a brighter glow. Ed looked at it and drew a deep breath. The cold air seared his lungs. For a moment the snow seemed to hesitate. Ahead he saw the dark break in the land, a wide cleft in the whiteness. The gelding lifted its head and snorted, blowing twin freshets of brume through its distended nostrils.

"Be gawdammed," Ed exclaimed. "The Rosebud, for certain sure."

He angled toward the dull silver-gray stream, then pulled up short, his eyes widening as they looked down at the snow-covered ground in front of him.

Two sets of horses' tracks crossed the trail. He recognized one of them. Snow had not yet filled them in completely, so they were still fresh. The tracks were made by one of his own horses, the one that Elaine Conroy had taken when she escaped.

Ed grinned. Maybe he wouldn't have to tell Taggart that Brant and the girl had gotten away, after all. Maybe Dan Brant's luck had run out at last. He drew a deep breath, unmindful of the sharp chill.

Now he had a track to follow, a clear, strong trail. Now the storm worked in his favor. He was the hunter, the quarry unaware that he was right behind them. The tracks, he figured, could not be more than fifteen minutes old.

On the snowy ground, his horse's hooves made no sound as he took up the trail, unable to quell his growing excitement.

Dan Brant might not die slow, as Taggart would have wished, thought Ed Rankin, but he would die even so. And he'd have the Conroy gal back, without Taggart ever knowing anything about her escape.

Ed lowered his head, rode into the teeth of the

storm. Gradually, the tracks grew fresher, their edges crisper, not yet rounded by the blowing snow.

Soon, he thought. Very soon.

Rankin, because of his elation at finding the tracks, and because of the storm, did not see another set of hoofprints eight or ten feet to the left of those he recognized.

These tracks were made by a pony. An Indian pony.

The pony was unshod and the drifting snow filled its tracks like sugar in an hourglass.

Ed Rankin never saw them.

Chapter Eight

The empty sockets of the skull stared up at them. Elaine Conroy shivered.

"Buffalo skull," Dan said, skirting it, his horse slightly spooked.

"Why is it there?"

The bleached mass of bone was sitting exactly in the center of the trail.

"It's there for me," he said.

Puzzled, Elaine watched him look closely at the skull. Then, he led out, following an imaginary line that extended from one horn. They both felt the wind rising, the chill that meant snow. A quarter of a mile away, Dan pulled up. There were three more skulls, arranged in a circle.

"I don't understand," she said.

"Gray Elk. He put them out for me. It's a signal. He knows we're here. We'll wait."

He swung down from the horse, and Elaine watched as he turned pale and almost fell to his knees.

"You're weak," she said. "Let me help you."

"Yes." He let her hold on to him for a moment, then he made his way to a tree and sat down slowly.

"Tie the horses up, will you, Elaine? I don't think we'll have to wait long."

"You're in no condition to travel anymore," she said. "You should let me make a shelter. There's a storm coming."

"I know. I have to meet Gray Elk. He can help."

His eyes closed with weariness. He shifted his weight to favor his wounded shoulder.

"I'm so sorry, Dan. For you. For Dennis. I know how close you were, even though you were so different from each other."

"Yes, we were different, inside, maybe. Outside, we looked the same. We both lost a good man. I'm sorry for you as well. You had to watch him die."

Elaine shuddered with remembrance.

"Did you . . . I mean . . . was he . . . ?" she stammered.

"I buried him proper, Elaine. No more need be said about it now. We can talk out our grief later."

"I'll tend to that wound now, while we're waiting," she said, a hint of command in her voice. Dan nodded and closed his eyes, listening for sound, letting his weariness wash over him like a tide.

Elaine saw that the wound was clean. The edges around the blue-black part were red and showed signs of hardening. She looked at Dan and marveled again at the uncanny resemblance he had to Dennis. Yet, she knew that the two men had been so different, as Dan had said, inside. They hadn't even seemed to be the same age. Dan always seemed older. Maybe that was because Dennis so obviously worshipped him. Maybe it was because Dan was a leader, Dennis a follower. Dennis liked to be with people. Dan seemed to be alone even in a crowd.

Her brother, Frank, had introduced Dennis to her less than two years before, in Denver. Dan was Frank's friend, but was driving another herd of cattle up from Texas at the time. Dennis was working in a dry goods store. He was very polite, a trifle shy, and terribly handsome. She hadn't thought anyone could be that handsome until she had met Dennis's twin brother, Dan. She had very nearly gone into shock. No one had bothered to tell her that the men were twins. She had just assumed that Dan was an older brother. They didn't make much of their being identical.

Elaine had chosen to marry Dennis and start her own ranch in Montana Territory. She didn't regret her decision, but had to fight hard to keep from feeling sorry for herself now that Dennis was dead, her dreams shattered. Dan was hurt and Frank was in danger. She had expected none of this. Yet Elaine was not a woman to bemoan her fate. She was determined to see things through as best she could. Right now Dan needed her attention. The wound was bound to fester unless he received some sort of treatment. It might even become infected. He could die if that happened.

"This wound needs a poultice on it," she said.

"Later," Dan told her. "At least the bleeding's stopped."

She tied a loose bandage around the wound and sat down to wait with Dan. The wind kept rising, and soon a few flakes of snow began to blow against her face. The wind dropped, and she wasn't as cold as before. Dan seemed to be dozing, but she knew he was alert because he heard the Indian long before she did. She watched Dan open his eyes and look through the trees.

At first she saw only a shadow. Then a shape. She gasped and slapped a hand against her mouth. The man wore a single eagle feather, sticking out of his dark black hair. He was wrapped in a robe that appeared to be made of antelope. He carried a rifle. Dan got to his feet slowly and waited for the warrior to ride up.

"*Hunh!*" said the Indian.

"*How, Cola,*" Dan grunted.

She heard a spatter of guttural language. The two men used their hands in a graceful talk, augmenting their speech. Dan's movements were not as fluid as the Indian's, and twice he clutched his throbbing shoulder.

She watched them, fascinated. The Sioux smelled of earth and grease and smoke and animal hide. She admired his beaded moccasins as he sat astride his painted pony. His cheekbones were high and his skin stretched tightly over them. He was very young, his eyes like polished beads. His talk, though harsh in his throat, had a musical quality to it, almost chanting. Dan's dialect seemed little different to her, deeper, more raspy perhaps.

"*Hiyapo!*" the Indian said.

"Let's mount up, Elaine," ordered Dan. "This is Flying Crow. He's going to take us to Gray Elk."

Elaine brought the horses. Dan got up in the saddle as though he had no wound.

87

The Indian turned his horse and the two followed him.

"What did he say?" she wanted to know.

"He wondered what you were doing here."

"Why, he never even looked at me."

"I told him you were medicine. Good medicine."

She looked sharply at Dan. She thought she could see the trace of a grin on his face.

"Where are we going?"

"To the Rosebud. It's not far. Gray Elk is waiting there. He's camped some distance above the trail, but he knows we've had some trouble, I gather. Some of the braves have been keeping account of us."

"I see," she said without understanding at all. She wanted to say more, but didn't know how to broach it without offending Dan. Still, she was determined to find out something that had bothered her for a long time. It had resurfaced since the arrival of the Indian brave.

"Don't follow in Flying Crow's tracks," Dan said to Elaine. "Stay eight or ten feet to the right."

"Why?" she asked.

"If someone's tracking us in this storm, he'll look at our tracks real hard. He won't be looking to the side. Even if he does, he won't be able to see much. That pony of Flying Crow's is unshod. The wind and snowdrift will blow away his tracks sooner than ours."

"I would never have thought of such a thing," said Elaine. "Do you think someone is following us?"

"Could be. I get a knife between my shoulder blades."

"What does that mean?"

88

"It's a feeling you get. If you're in the woods much, or if you pay attention in a town. Someone stares at you, you feel it. Someone wants to shoot you in the back, you feel that knife."

"You're a very odd man, Daniel. Most people don't think about such things."

"No, most don't," he said.

They rode ten or twelve feet to the right of Flying Crow, following him, but not blending their tracks with his. They followed blindly, because the snow blew down a swirl of thin flakes on the land and they had no bearings.

The small dry flakes powdered the trail. The air began to moisten and the temperature crept lower. Gelid fingers probed through their coats on the knifing wind.

The snow began to fall in thick flakes, packing onto the ground. Gradually, the sounds of the horses' hooves began to muffle. Flying Crow seemed to be in no hurry. Dan and Elaine followed him along a game trail that was wide enough for two horses side by side.

Elaine waited as long as she could.

"How can you be friends to these—these savages?" she asked.

Dan shot her a look that chilled her.

"I mean, after what you went through."

She knew what had happened. Dennis had told her one day. The Brant family had traveled from Illinois out to this country. Their wagon train had been ambushed. Many of the people had been killed. Dan had been captured, their parents killed. Dennis had escaped with another family and gotten back to

Cherry Creek. Dan had lived with the Sioux for four years. He had been sixteen when this had happened. He was twenty-two now. The memory should still be fresh in his mind.

"There was nothing personal in it," Dan said to her. "We were intruders. If a tribe of Sioux had come into our lands in Illinois, we probably would have shot them all dead. We're still the intruders, but we've got the advantage now. The Sioux's days are numbered. They know that. Gray Elk was my friend. He still is."

"Maybe he killed your parents."

"Maybe. That was a long time ago. The Sioux believe the Great Spirit gave them this land. They think more of it than the white man does, or think they do. The Brants came out here too soon, before the land was settled. They were always that way, even back in Ireland. We were always ahead of the rest of the bunch. In a few years the Sioux will be pushed into a corner like the eastern tribes. They won't give up their lands easily, but they will give them up. There are too many of us."

"You came here. Frank did. To live. Yet you sound sad."

"I am sad. I wish the Indian could stay. I wish we could live together in peace."

"Can't you?"

"As individuals, perhaps. Yes, we could. We could learn things from each other. But the army backs up the settlers. The army breaks the government's treaties. The Indian has no government to fall back on, no reserves. He is all instinct. He doesn't understand the white man's need to own land. He doesn't understand lumber or minerals or farming. The Indian is a rover, a hunter. He does not understand how a white man can own land that was given to the Indian. It's sad but true."

"You and Frank want to live here. So did Dennis. Why?"

"Because it's good land. A lot of it still unspoiled. I stay here only because the Sioux let me, though. If they told me to go, I would leave."

"Other white settlers would come in. Your going would make no difference."

"Yes, they would come. They're coming now. The army may close the Bozeman, but the settlers will find another way. The Sioux know this, but they have decided to close the roads that violate the sacred Paha Sapa, the Black Hills. They think this will stop the flood of whites onto their land."

"But it won't."

"No, Elaine, it won't."

She looked at Dan with new respect. She hadn't realized the depth of his feelings before. She had always pictured him as a hard-driving cattleman, more action than thought. Yet there was obviously a deeper side to Dan that she never suspected until now.

"Why didn't you build your ranch in Colorado?" she asked abruptly.

Dan looked at her a long time before answering.

"I like this land," he said. "I spent the best years of my life here."

She wondered how he could say such a thing when the circumstances were so grim. She had always thought he was an unwilling prisoner of the Sioux, but now she realized that this wasn't entirely true. Looking at him now, she wondered how much of the wildness was still in him. He rode like Flying Crow, who was ahead of them. She wondered if he thought like him too.

The snow began to thicken as the wind dropped. Elaine felt warmer than she had before. Dan had given her his sheepskin coat and a pair of gloves. She was grateful and knew that he must be cold himself, wearing only a light jacket over his wool shirt. The snow was sticking to the ground fast now, and the horses were batting the flakes out of their eyes with fluttering eyelashes.

Still, Flying Crow seemed to be in no particular hurry. At times, Dan and Elaine had to follow single file. There was no avoiding it along the narrow stretches. The brave picked his way carefully along the game trail. His horse's unshod hooves made little sound on the snow that was piling up fast. He seemed no more than a shadow in front of them at times. Elaine rode in front of Dan, who brought up the rear now that they were through talking. They crossed small trickles of water, tiny streams running into the Rosebud. They gained altitude, threading through the fir and spruce, the stunted juniper. One juniper was shattered where a bull elk had set his mighty rack against its branches, shredding it with repeated thrusts of its sharp tines.

Finally, the Indian stopped. Below, they heard the Rosebud gurgling its way, surging against the banks with melted snow swelling its volume. Dan rode up to Flying Crow.

"Gray Wolf is there," the Indian said in Lakota,

pointing.

"*Hunh!*" Dan grunted.

The Indian rode north, then east. Dan watched him go, waiting while the snow filled the tracks.

"What is it, Dan? Why did he leave?"

"He's going back to his camp. Something's up. Gray Wolf has his camp over yonder, in that clump of lodgepole pine and spruce."

"Why all the secrecy?"

"I don't know, Elaine. It could be dangerous for us. For Gray Elk too."

He could smell it, almost. When Flying Crow's tracks were obliterated by the snow, he moved toward where the Indian had pointed, two hundred yards ahead, close to the Rosebud. Elaine followed, bewildered. She saw Dan's hand touch the butt of his pistol, and she frowned. It was so quiet and still, and everything was white around her.

They moved into the trees. Dan stopped and listened.

A shape moved out ahead of them.

Elaine gasped when she saw the tall Indian. He wore a buffalo-horn hat and the robes flowed down from his wide shoulders. He held a rifle in his hand, an eagle feather tied to its stock. He raised his other hand, palm out, in greeting. Dan rode up to him, waving Elaine back.

"Stay here," he said.

She watched as the two men spoke. She tried to figure out the signs that Gray Elk made with his hands. They were like graceful birds moving in rapid flight. After a while Dan rode back to her.

"Trouble?" she asked.

"Could be. The Sioux may be getting ready for war. Gray Elk wouldn't tell me everything. He may not know all there is to know about it. I sensed that his tribe is running out of patience. It is very dangerous for whites here, and he can offer us no protection."

"What shall we do?"

"I told him we were going to the B Bar C. I also told him that the cattle were his, but that I wanted the men who took them myself. He said they had let the cattle through because of our brand being on them. He may not trust me under the circumstances. He has listened to so many lies from other white men, he may think I'm lying too. I don't like it, Elaine. But for the time being we are safe. I reckon they'll have a big powwow and then it might not be so good for us. Come, I want you to meet my friend."

She rode over to Gray Elk with Dan. He seemed even more imposing up close. She sensed the inner strength of the man, but he was powerfully built as well. She shuddered inwardly to think of what such a man must have done to whites who entered his lands. Gray Elk, despite his friendship with Dan, was still a savage. And even that friendship seemed to be on shaky ground at the moment.

"Elaine," he said to Gray Elk. Then in the Lakota tongue, "Sister. Good woman. Mine."

Gray Elk grunted. His hands made sign.

"Hello, good friend."

"We will go now," Dan told him. "We are followed. My heart soars because you are my friend."

"Yes. Gray Elk wishes that this will always be.

Now, go fast," said Gray Elk. "Many Lakota go to camp. Much talk."

"I will bring you the cattle," said Dan.

Gray Elk disappeared, his horse moving out of their sight soundless as a whisper.

"Such a quiet camp," Dan muttered.

"What do you mean?" she asked.

"No smoke, no noise. It is a war camp, I'm thinking."

"We had better leave. I still want to tend to your wound."

"Yes," he said. "We must go."

But he sat his horse motionless, thinking of the changes that were bound to come. Now it seemed even more important that he get those stolen cattle to Gray Elk. He wondered, though, if under the circumstances, he was doing the right thing. Gray Elk, it seemed, might no longer be a friend, but an enemy.

Three hundred yards away, on foot, Ed Rankin watched them from under the snow-flocked branches of a spruce. He was well hidden; no one could see him from his vantage point. His horse was some distance away, a feedbag on so that he wouldn't whinny. There was a hatful of grain in the bag. Ed breathed into his coat so that his breath wouldn't show. He was a patient man and a careful one. Snow melted on the barrel of his rifle as the flakes fell. He had some waiting to do, but when Brant and the girl moved, so would he.

Chapter Nine

The shot came from far away, muffled by the falling snow. Dan kicked his horse into action. Elaine's leapt from sheer excitement. They rode toward the sound of the shot.

Ed Rankin brought his rifle down from his shoulder. He had not fired. Someone else had done so. Damn! The other shot had saved Dan's life. Ed had been about to squeeze the trigger when Dan had bolted out of his sights.

"Damn," he muttered. He slogged through the snow back to where his horse was tied. Now he'd have to track Dan all over again. To add to the danger, there were Sioux along the Rosebud. Ed felt a prickly sensation under his scalp. It was a long walk to where he'd left his horse. If he didn't hurry, the snow would fill up the tracks before he could get on their trail again. If the wind came up, it would be worse. He wondered who had been shooting. The shot was too far away to tell.

* * *

Dan rode fast, jerking his Hawken free of its scabbard. Breathless, Elaine followed, ducking the branches of trees that threatened to unseat her. They topped a rise and came riding down to an open spot. Some distance away there was a dark spot in the snow. A spotted pony stood several yards off, trailing its reins. Elaine pulled her horse up short. Dan rode over to the figure sprawled in the snow. He dismounted.

"It's Flying Crow," he called to Elaine.

"Is he dead?"

"Yes." There was a bullet hole in the Sioux's back. Dan knew that he had died instantly. The snow beneath his body was rusty with spilled blood. The exit hole in his chest was large. He laid the dead warrior back down in the snow. His eyes followed a line from the wound into the trees. He mounted his horse and rode back to Elaine.

"The trouble will come soon now," he told her.

They rode to the place where Dan had looked. A man had stood there. A white man by the boot tracks.

"He shot Flying Crow in the back."

"Why?"

"Because he was an Indian," Dan said coldly. "He was in no danger. Flying Crow didn't even know he was here."

Elaine looked at Dan. There was a dark and terrible look on his face. Something pulled at her senses; something shriveled inside her stomach. His eyes seemed to flash fire. A muscle in his face twitched. She could almost hear his teeth grinding together inside his tight-lipped mouth. She saw the man and his rifle. They were joined together into a single piece of sculpture.

"God help him," she said involuntarily.

"Flying Crow? He's beyond help."

"No," Elaine said quietly. "The man who was here."

Dan swung off through the snow, following the tracks. Elaine had no choice but to follow. The sky was darkening and she was hungry, but Dan was possessed, she knew. She could sense his determination by the broad expanse of his back. He seemed to her like a rock bent on starting an avalanche. She began to realize why Dennis had worshipped him. There was a feeling of determination and raw power in Dan's presence. She would never forget the awesome look on his face when he had seen the tracks of the bushwhacker. She wondered if he wasn't half savage after having lived with the Sioux for those four years.

The tracks were easy to follow. The horseman had ridden fast in his flight away from the murder scene. Blobs of snow were scattered on both sides of the deep holes gouged by the running horse. There was a place where the horse had slid, climbing up through brush away from the Rosebud. There were holes where chunks of snow had fallen from evergreen boughs to mark the passage of man and beast. The tracks veered off to the left, heading back to the Bozeman. Dan wasted no time, but prodded his mount to move faster into the blinding veil of snow that threatened to block his vision as the shadows of day set up stakes to the west that grew longer with every passing moment.

The tracks became fresher and fresher. Dan slowed his horse. Behind him, Elaine panted for breath. He stopped his horse and waited for her.

"I want you to ride to the Rosebud and wait," he told her. "Down there."

She looked where he was pointing.

"Why?"

"He's circling. I don't want you in the way."

"Am I in the way?" A flash of resentment sparked her eyes.

"You could be," he said curtly. "Hurry. He's very close."

"Be careful, Dan," she said, suddenly concerned. "I'm totally lost out here."

"I'll be back. Wait by the Rosebud, under shelter. I'll whistle when I come back, so you'll know it's me."

He watched her until she was safely away from him, then continued tracking. He knew that the man was circling to come up behind him. There was nothing he could do for a time, except follow. The tracks were so fresh, he was sure he was within earshot of the man he pursued. He picked his way carefully, stopping often to listen. Visibility was only a few feet now as the snowflakes continued to fall in thick, relentless streamers. He rode on until he saw where the tracks curved up to the high ground to his left. There was a gully there, a place where a man could find concealment.

He knew he had to make a decision. He could widen the circle and come up on the other side of the deep gully. Or, he could backtrack and wait for his man. There was a chance he was holed up in the gully, but Dan bet that this wasn't the case. Somehow he had the feeling that the man was tracking him, knew that he was close by. It was just a feeling, but it was strong enough to make Dan do a dangerous thing.

He rode on for a few more yards, then slid silently out of the saddle. A man afoot in such country was asking for trouble. He could easily fall victim to wild animals, Indians, or the weather. Yet it was a chance he had to take. Even so, Dan figured he had the advantage. He was the hunter, and he knew how to hunt.

The horse stepped off a few yards, stopped, and looked back at him. Dan ignored the plea in the animal's eyes. He took off his hat and waved it. The horse went a few steps more. Dan began to backtrack and circle toward the gully. He used the trees for cover, moving between them at intervals, listening for sounds in between.

He remembered his first deer, back in Illinois. He had been only fourteen, but he had been hunting since he was eight. The November woods had crackled with leaves and deer. He had followed the fresh tracks of what appeared to be a big buck. He carried his first good rifle, a flintlock made by Henry Leman of Lancaster, Pennsylvania. He, Dennis, and their father had gone to the factory on Miffland Street, west of Duke, a part of Leman's father's brewery. Dan and Dennis were young when they started hunting, but the senior Brant believed in thinking ahead. Dan loved that graceful Pennsylvania rifle, and the memory of his first buck was equally important in his mind.

That's when he had learned that a hunted animal will often double back to get a look at its pursuer. He had been so busy tracking the deer that he hadn't noticed that it was circling, skulking through the woods like a rabbit. Something, perhaps instinct, had made him stop and wait. The buck had come along, following his spoor. Dan raised his Leman rifle and touched the trigger. The flint struck the closed frizzen. A shower of sparks flew into the pan. There was a puff of smoke and then an explosion. The rifled ball had gone true, straight to the buck's chest, exploding its lungs. Later, he went over the tracks to see if it had been the same buck he'd been following. He had learned a valuable lesson that day. The buck had been the one he'd tracked.

And now a man was doubling back on him. So, too, was he doubling back on the man. Dan knew the risks involved but knew, as well, he had no choice. The man he was tracking had killed at least once. He had shot another man, an Indian, but a man nonetheless, in the back. He had no wish to die in such a manner. This way he could at least face his adversary. Then let the better man win. This was part of his code, the only one he knew. Death was inevitable, but it need not happen through carelessness.

Dan kept low and moved quietly, still hunting. He thought of the man as a deer, as prey. He also thought of him as someone hunting him, with the ability and means to kill. He moved up through the trees, listening, stepping carefully. He waited a long time between moves, flattening himself against a tree, presenting no silhouette, no target.

The pain in his shoulder began to throb again. The cold seemed to seek out the wound and sear it with its frosty probe. He was hungry. He worried about Elaine, who must also be needing nourishment. There was not much left of the day; the shadows broadened and lengthened in the maze of trees where he wound his way.

It took him only a short time to reach the gully, but it seemed long. That was something he had learned from the Sioux. Move as little as possible. Nothing quick. He had stalked both antelope and prairie chickens. He had learned how to be part of the landscape, to move only when it was possible to move without being seen. Now, however, there was a gun waiting for him at the end of the stalk. He moved even more carefully than he would have if stalking game.

He reached the gully and waited.

The snow falling had a soporific effect on him. He shook it off mentally. It was quiet, but that made listening all the more important. He must not miss any sound. His eyes scanned the whiteness, the broken ground. He blinked to shut out the light, strengthen his eyes. He looked for tracks on the opposite slope. The fading light was tricky. A man could see things that weren't there.

He was glad the wind was down. Still, the snowflakes were so thick that his vision was limited. He moved to another tree, took another angle of sight on the gully. It narrowed out of view, yet he knew it would be suicide to steal out for a further look.

It was time to wait.

He let the snow cling to him as it fell. He became

part of the tree. He hugged it, with his rifle up against it, ready to bring down for a quick snap shot. He checked behind him and to the sides. He was protected from ambush in those three directions. His man would have to come to him from the front. There was the chance, of course, that the one he hunted would make a wider circle, but Dan didn't think he would. The gully was long enough so the backshooter would have to cross it at some point. Dan was betting that he had intercepted the point of crossing to within a few yards.

He was conscious of his own breathing. He kept his mouth closed and drew the air in through his nose. There was no telltale puff of steam issuing from his mouth. He watched the snow build up, the gully lose its depth, its sides. He marked every bush he could see, let his eyes become accustomed to the dark shapes amid the white, shapes building up faster and faster.

He heard a branch crack on the farthest slope, above him.

He drew a deep breath and cocked an ear in the direction of the sound. The silence became eerie, maddening. Still, that had been enough. He was in the right place. A few moments later he heard a horse snorting. His eyes burned from peering into the bleak, floury depths of the snowfall. He wiped snow from his front sight, looked down his barrel. The rear sight was clean, the lock and hammer dry where they rested next to his chest. He held the rifle so the muzzle wouldn't block up with snow. He had no wish to plug his barrel and ring it. Such things happened. He had seen men blow barrels up by not seating the ball over the charge properly. A twig, a collection of snow, could do the same thing.

There was another sound. This one was more elusive. It sounded like a blanket being dragged over a floor. Or a man wading through deep sand.

Or a horse moving slow through thick snow.

Dan had to force himself not to stiffen up, to stifle the tautness creeping into his belly like a tightening cinch. This was not a time for buck fever. He blinked his eyes again and let his breath flow back to normal. He was very careful not to move. He was one with the tree.

He heard the horse whicker not far away. A moment later he heard the sound of leather creaking. He strained his ears and heard the flap of reins.

The man was dismounting.

It would not be long now. Dan squeezed the trigger of his rifle and cocked the hammer back silently. He eased the hammer back to normal position. The cocking had made only a small, muffled sound. There was a trigger for a hair touch, but he didn't set it. It would be too tricky with the cold and his gloves. Once the hair trigger was set, it would take only a slight touch to set it off. Also there was no way to control the audible click for the set trigger. It made little noise, but keen ears could detect if from some distance.

And, too, he was not a bushwhacker. He wanted to see the man, wanted to give him a chance while keeping the edge.

There was a long silence. Dan felt as if he were inside a white cocoon, a silent, snowy world where no sound could penetrate. It was only an illusion, he knew. His ears were tuned to larger sounds, sounds louder than the soft thunk of snow on branches, on his jacket and hat. If the man made a mistake, if he stumbled, or coughed, or scratched, Dan was sure that he would hear such sounds.

But the silence was unnerving. The longer it continued, the more he doubted the sounds he had heard before. Had he only imagined them? Such was the power of the mind, he thought ruefully. In this whiteness, all of the senses were distorted, suspect.

Dan thought that the man had outsmarted him. Yet, this was dangerous. He couldn't relax, couldn't move to check out his vagrant hunch. It was still best to wait. He had to wait.

Out of the corner of his eye he saw movement. It was only slight. He peered hard in the direction of the quick flash of dark that had caught his vision.

There! He saw it again!

A man's hat bobbed toward him over the crest of the gully's far ridge. There was little cover, and the hat began to move.

Dan brought his rifle down slightly, moving it slowly until the barrel rested at eye level.

He glimpsed the man's head, his shoulders, then his trunk. Finally, the man stalked down the slope. He stopped, raising his head.

"Rankin!" Dan yelled.

Todd Rankin, startled, raised his rifle and tried to find the source of the voice.

"What the . . . !" he exclaimed.

Dan stepped from behind the tree, his Hawken leveled at Todd.

"I'm just sorry as hell it isn't your rotten brother,"

Dan said, holding his sight on the man's chest.

Todd swung his rifle, a full second too late.

There was a droning chunk as Dan squeezed the trigger of the Hawken. A shower of sparks burned through the snow. Smoke mingled with the flakes like a miniature white cloud.

Todd fell backward, a bright rose flowering on his chest where the blood from his heart pumped a deep red fountain that soon darkened as it thickened.

Dan walked over to the fallen man and looked into his frosty eyes.

"That was for Flying Crow, you son of a bitch!"

Todd Rankin's eyes stayed open, but they couldn't see anything. Neither could his ears hear.

Dan was satisfied. His nostrils smarted from the stench of black powder. He poured a measured amount of powder down his barrel, wet a piece of cloth in his mouth, put it on the muzzle, and placed a round ball atop it. He rammed the ball down with a short starter and cut the patch off. He rammed the ball down farther, then took his ramrod and seated the ball. He capped the nipple of his rifle and turned away from the dead man.

He felt empty. Todd was only one of the men who had murdered his brother. It looked, in fact, as though he had been the least of them. He had died too easily, too quickly. Dan felt cheated somehow, yet he did not diminish this death. Todd had chosen to live by the gun, and so he died. But it was not a thing that Dan took lightly. A man's life was still worth something. It was too bad that Todd Rankin sold his so cheap.

Now he had to find his horse, get back to Elaine.

He hoped Gray Elk could read the sign. Flying Crow had been avenged, but there was no one to know it yet.

He drew a deep breath for the first time since the stalking began. But he knew he had to go on. Todd may not have been alone. Although he had not seen any other tracks, Todd could have ridden off by himself. The others may not have been far away. Yes, he had stayed too long. Elaine would have heard the shot, might be worried. He did not want to leave her alone, so near to the Sioux, too long.

Suddenly apprehensive, Dan began to run.

Chapter Ten

Ed Rankin checked himself from moving too quick.

He heard the shot that killed Flying Crow, saw Dan and Elaine disappear through the trees. He waited a long time before trying to follow, since he didn't know what he might run into. When he did leave, he made a wide sweep to the high ground, marking the direction the shot had come from, and allowing for it as he rode to a point where he could take a look at things, undetected.

It took him only a few moments to see what had happened. He was curious, though, about who had shot the Indian. He watched as Dan and Elaine tracked the ambusher. He wanted to follow them and was about to strike out on the trail when he saw another Indian ride up to the place. It was Gray Elk, but he didn't know the name of the warrior. He knew only that he looked important, a chief, perhaps. Ed was unable to move as long as the Indian was there, so he waited, watched.

The warrior dismounted and saw the tracks. He

uttered an unintelligible cry and looked in the direction where Dan and Elaine had ridden. He shook his rifle in the air and made a sign that Ed understood.

It was a sign to kill.

Then Gray Elk carried the body of the dead Indian to his horse and put him over the saddle. He walked off, leading his horse. He called out just as Ed was raising his own rifle for a shot. More Indians appeared and Ed lowered his rifle. He heard snatches of their conversation but could make nothing out of it. One of the braves dismounted and gave his reins to Gray Elk.

While they were busy talking and gesticulating, Ed rode off, slow, circling to intersect Dan Brant's trail.

He knew Dan Brant hadn't killed the Indian, but he had a hunch the Indians didn't know that. There was a chance the tall warrior might do his job for him. In the meantime, he had to make sure Dan was accounted for—and the girl too. When he thought he was far enough away from the gathered Sioux, he stepped up his pace. He crossed Brant's tracks and began following cautiously.

The shot brought him up short.

It came from a different direction than he had expected—not straight ahead, but off to the left, higher up. He left the tracks and rode up in the direction of the gunshot.

The sound of the shot, he knew, had little chance of carrying back to the Indians. The snowfall was too thick. Or, at least, he hoped it was. Something had happened and he had to find out what it was. Either Dan had been shot, or he had shot someone. Who?

His horse floundered up the slope to the ridge, its hooves slipping on the loose wet snow. He continued riding past the top of the gully until he ran into a set of horse's tracks. These were heading down into the gully. He looked at the tracks closely. He started to shake as he realized that he was following his son's tracks. He tried to stop the shaking, but the premonition persisted. There had been but a single shot. One man possibly lay dead in the snow. Would it be Todd or Dan Brant?

Ed was not so cautious now. He knew he was following a trail that led to death. He felt a numbness creeping into his sensibilities that was not of the cold. He was trying to steel himself for what he might find in the heart of the gully. The snow blew into his face and eyes, but he paid it little mind. Something seemed to be swelling in his chest, and he found it difficult to breathe.

He rode into the gully and saw the sorrel standing hipshot, its back to the lightly blowing snow. He felt a wrench in his stomach, and his hands on the reins seemed to lose all feeling. He made out the fast-fading tracks and continued on his way, an invisible band tightening around his chest. The breathing came even harder.

He saw the figure sprawled in the snow and knew it was Todd.

Ed dismounted even before he got to the body. He staggered to it and saw the face, first. It was white as the snow that half covered it. He knelt down and brushed the flakes from Todd's dead eyes, off his cheeks and lips. It was then that he saw the hole in his son's chest, dark and ugly. Despite himself, tears came to his eyes.

"Todd!" he screamed, and his cry fell in the muffled gully like a mossy stone on thick grass.

Ed picked his son up by the shoulders and held him tight against his chest. Tears stung his eyes.

"Todd," he crooned, "he done kilt you, boy. Why? Why'd you let him, Todd boy?"

He squeezed the tears out of his eyes and loosened his grip on his son.

"This haint no place to die, Todd. You shoulda lived to be as old as me, die on a porch some'eres where the sun was warm on your face. Your ma won't like this none and hit's all my doin'. I'm gonna git the man what done this, Todd. You can be sartin sure of that."

It was useless, and Ed knew it. He just couldn't help himself. Joe was wounded and now Todd was dead. All because of him. He didn't feel very big at that moment.

The tightness in his chest began to go away, replaced by a burning anger, a violent hatred of Dan Brant.

"He kilt you, Todd. Dan Brant. I'll git him for ya. He'll draw few breaths I'm thinkin' afore he jines up with ye."

Ed laid his son back down in the snow and looked at his quiet face, the closed eyes, for a long time as the flakes continued to fall. He stood up and looked around. He saw a likely spot to place his boy to rest and walked over to the brush. He moved it aside and began clearing the snow away. He carried Todd's body over to the dry ground and folded his hands on his chest. He loosened Todd's pistol belt and took it

111

off, slung it over his shoulder. He walked over and picked up Todd's rifle.

"I'll keep these, boy, in 'membrance of ye."

He put the weapons on his horse and went back covered the body with brush. He knew it was not good enough, but he was hoping the snowfall would hide Todd long enough so that the Indians wouldn't get to him. The coyotes or wolves would, in time, no matter what he did. His hands were cold and his face felt raw, as though he'd just shaved with cold water. He stood there by the makeshift grave for a long time until the snow covered up enough of Todd to satisfy him.

He mounted his horse, then went and got the sorrel. He tipped his hat in Todd's direction as he rode away, following the depressions in the snow that marked the trail of Dan and Elaine. He led the sorrel and looked down at his son's pistol belt every now and then, a deep sadness soaking through him.

The night began to close in around him as he neared the Bozeman Trail. There was no hurry now. He knew where Dan and Elaine were headed. He would sleep light and get started early in the morning. He would be headed, the same as they, for the B Bar C. The only difference was, Ed knew what was waiting for him—Zeb Taggart and the rest of the bunch. The thought gave him comfort as he found shelter and bedded down for the night, the tears in his eyes long dried and left on his backtrail, the same as Todd.

Gray Elk, Shadow, Iron Knife, and Lame Hawk

found Todd's body at twilight. There was not much left of it when they finished cutting off various parts. The snow was bloody for yards around. The Lakota warriors were in a frenzy. Shadow, Nagin in Lakota, and Lame Hawk, Cetan Huste, were all for calling down the entire tribe on the new fort built on the Rosebud, slaughtering all the soldiers there. Iron Knife, Mila Maza, wanted to follow the tracks of Flying Crow's killers and count coups on them. Gray Elk said that he knew where to find the killers of Flying Crow and said that they should go back to the camp and make preparations, gather more friends to go with them.

The men held a long and heated council.

There was a compromise. Gray Elk, Iron Knife, and Shadow would follow the trail of the long knives. Lame Hawk would go back to camp and try to get two dozen warriors to ride with them. They gave *hunhs* of assent, and split up.

Iron Knife carried Todd's genitals with him.

Shadow took his heart.

Gray Elk carried the bloody scalp thonged to his rifle.

They, too, headed for the B Bar C, following three sets of tracks, one set very recent.

Dan was exhausted, but he rode at a trot, following the tracks in the snow.

Elaine waited where he told her to and watched him until the snowfall closed behind him like a curtain.

Dan flushed the rabbit and slid out of his saddle,

his rifle in hand. The rabbit started to circle and Dan whistled. The rabbit stopped even as Dan brought his Hawken up to his shoulder. He held just below its ear, on the neck, and drew a deep breath, held it. He squeezed the trigger very gently.

There was a loud crack and a puff of smoke. The lead ball caught the rabbit square in the head, blowing it apart. The rabbit leapt up into the air and flopped down into the snow, its hind feet kicking spasmodically. Fresh blood stained the snow red.

Dan went to the rabbit and reloaded his rifle as he stood over the convulsive animal.

"Thank you, my brother," he said in the Lakota tongue. "You will feed me now. Someday my flesh will feed the earth that feeds your brothers. Forgive me for killing you. We must eat."

It was something he had learned from the Sioux. No game was killed without an apology. Nothing of the earth was harmed without mentioning the connection between all living things. To the Indians, everything was alive, even the rocks.

He picked up the rabbit and, with his knife, deftly skinned it and cleaned it. He wrapped the fresh carcass, along with the heart, liver, and kidneys, in the skin and put the bundle into his pocket. He left the entrails in the snow to feed whatever animal might come by.

It was getting dark and he knew they would have to keep moving awhile longer. He had to make a fire to cook the rabbit, and he didn't want to be surprised by anyone who might be following them. He found Elaine waiting for him, shivering in the cold.

"We'll move on down for a ways," he said.

"I'm exhausted, Dan. Can't we make a camp now?"

"No. Our tracks are still fresh behind us. Come on."

She was mildly surprised at his sudden curtness. But then, she had never known him really well. He was just the brother of her betrothed. She had wanted his approval, but never felt she had gotten it. Maybe she had been expecting too much from a half savage, barely civilized man. She repressed the urge to argue and, gritting her teeth, followed him on a path parallel to the Rosebud.

The snow was frightening to her. She felt as though she were in a tunnel. The light grew dimmer as they rode on, and she kept looking back to see if anyone was following them. Soon she could barely see the rump of Dan's horse and she stopped looking over her shoulder. She felt relief when he finally stopped in a thick clump of spruce that made a natural, somewhat ragged circle. Inside the shelter, the snow was not so thick, and the trees would mask a small fire.

"We'll eat here," he told her, dismounting.

"Won't we stop for the night? It's getting so dark."

"No, we'll get some nourishment and camp farther down. Here there will be light from the fire and the smells, fair invitation for unwanted company."

"Dan, I—I can't go on much longer."

"Tie up your horse, Elaine, and don't whine."

"I'm not whining," she said indignantly.

"Good. I'm glad to hear it. I'll build us a fire and cook this rabbit. It's little enough, but it'll have to do."

She wanted to curse him at that moment, but she held her tongue.

Dan didn't waste time. He cleared the snow away from the ground, making a small circle for dry brush. He walked out of the circle, gathered squaw wood, the thin dead branches growing on the pines below the new branches. The squaw wood was dry and made for good tinder. He gathered deadwood, the driest he could find, and brought it into their temporary shelter. He made a small pile of the squaw wood, took flint and striking steel from his possibles bag, and started the fire. He blew on the tinder until the tiny blaze caught the larger bits of squaw wood. He piled up bigger and bigger kindling until the glaze was sufficient to go on its own. He cut two forked sticks from saplings he found along the river, stuck them into the ground on two sides of the fire, and pounded them in solid. He cut another straight stick and skewered the rabbit on it and placed this between the forked sticks, over the fire. He kept the heart, liver, and kidneys inside the rabbit skin and put this into the fire after it was going well.

Elaine hunkered next to the fire, watching Dan, who seemed oblivious to her. He seemed even more savage to her since the recent events. He was as wild as the Indians who lived in the hills and plains around them. Yet the resemblance to Dennis was uncanny. She was unnerved by the likeness, something in her wanting to reach out to him as she had to Dennis. She warmed her hands over the licking flames. The snow seemed to be beaten back, momentarily, by the fire, but she knew it was only an illusion. The darkness drew even closer around them.

The smell from the roasting rabbit made her realize how hungry she was. The drippings struck the fire, hissed, made the wood pop and crackle. She watched as Dan turned the animal on the spit, the flames licking at the flesh but never lingering for more than a second or two. Her mouth watered. She had eaten rabbit before, but never in such primitive fashion. When it was done and Dan cut her off a tender foreleg, she ate it eagerly. He handed her his canteen and she drank from it. She ate another portion as he pulled the cooked liver, heart, and gizzard from the flames. He offered the morsels to her.

"No, thanks," she said. "I'm getting quite full."

Dan ate the back and hindquarters and the innards, staring at the darkness instead of at the fire. He pushed snow onto the dying embers when he was finished and stood up.

"We have to move," he said. He was restless again, wondering if they had not stayed too long in this one spot. It was just a feeling, but he had had such feelings before. More than once, his hunches had saved his life. He felt that way now, a stirring in him to be on the move, to leave this place of relative comfort behind.

"Do we? Who could be following us? It's very quiet now, and the snow's quite deep."

"I don't know. A lot happened back there. Depends on who reads the sign and how they read it."

"What do you mean?"

"Those Sioux back there might think I killed Flying Crow, for one thing. If they read the sign real careful, they won't make that mistake. But those are hot-blooded Oglala braves and they might not look too hard when all they can see is white men at the base of their troubles."

"But you are their friend."

"Was. Maybe they don't want my friendship any more. Besides, it's not only the Sioux we might have to worry about."

"What?"

"I killed Todd Rankin. His pa, or his brother, Joe, might be following my track. Somebody might just want to come onto this fire and catch us by surprise. I would if I were hunting a man real hard. Ed Rankin, Todd's pa, would be hunting me real hard if he knows I killed his son."

"I don't understand you, Dan. It's going to be hard enough to keep warm without going any farther."

"Elaine, I don't ask you to understand me. I'm not Dennis and I can't see why he'd take up with a woman, no offense to you. We were different from the start. I got you on my hands now, and I'll deliver you to your brother safe and sound if I can. After that I think you'd best look to your own self. Until then, though, I got to call the shots."

Stunned, Elaine looked at him, his face invisible through the falling snow. He was only a silhouette among the shadows of the spruce trees.

"You sound as though you resent me, as though you didn't approve of my marrying your brother!"

"Maybe. I think he was paying attention to the wrong thing on this drive. He might be alive today if he'd not had you with him."

Elaine walked up to Dan and looked up at him.

trying to see his face.

"You think that!" she exclaimed. "You think your brother died because he was with me?"

"It's possible," Dan said quietly. "It's a thought that crossed my mind."

"You . . . you're not being fair," she stammered, but she felt so stricken she could not continue.

Elaine turned away from him, glad he couldn't see the tears that welled up in her eyes.

She was further humiliated when he, mounted, took her reins and led her to the place where they would camp that night. Why, she thought, he was acting as if she could not guide her own mount. He wasn't being fair. It seemed he meant to humiliate her even more by such actions. A soft tinge of vermilion bloomed on her cheeks like a sudden rash. Sometimes men were such blockheads. Dan was an exasperating man. She wondered why she felt more of a prisoner with him than she had with the Rankins.

Elaine forgot about her weariness as a quiet rage began to build within her. Her cheeks flared red, as if her face had been scoured with flame at the blacksmith's forge.

Chapter Eleven

"The cattle's jumpy as grasshoppers and Taggart's bunch ain't nowheres near them," Lou Hardy said.

"You checked?" Frank Conroy stood in the doorway of the log house, rifle in hand. He was not a tall man, but burly, round-shouldered, easy on his feet, his pear-shaped face ruddy from the wind and blowing snow, blue eyes sparkling like cut gems. He wore a cap-'n'-ball revolver and a hunting knife on his belt.

"Yep," said Lou, a tall, angular man, hard as an oak slab, high-cheekboned, similarly armed. "Jimmy and Hank are keepin' an eye on the Taggart outfit. I think someone's up in the hills."

"You think they might be trying to come in the back way?"

" 'Pears that way."

"We'll sit tight. It could be Dan. He knows the way in here from that direction."

"It's what I was thinkin'," said Hardy, who missed the warmth of a Texas ranch.

"At least it's stopped snowing," said Frank, clos-

120

ing the door. The two men walked to the back of the house and looked up at the hills. Frank was older than Dan and Dennis, and Elaine; he was almost thirty. "It's my guess that if it's Dan up there, he'll come in after dark. We'll take turns watching from this direction. I don't want any surprises from Taggart."

"They may try and run the cattle off tonight, snow or no snow."

"Could be," said Frank. "Jimmy and Hank couldn't handle them."

"Nope. They got too many men."

"I wasn't expecting Dan and Dennis until tomorrow or the next day. Maybe the day after if they dropped off the cattle at Gray Elk's camp."

"The snow could hold 'em up more."

"You want the first watch, Lou?"

"I'll take it. Bring me some grub after a while, will ya?"

"I'll see to the stew. The Wiley kid can take grub to Jimmy and Hank."

The Wiley kid was a drifter who'd come there a month before, starving and willing to work. Frank had felt sorry for him and put him up. Jimmy and Hank were two Texans who had come up the trail with Lou. Jimmy Carter and Hank Niles. No one knew the Wiley kid's first name. They just called him Wiley. He was about nineteen, give or take a year. As the two men talked, he was feeding the horses in the corral built in a natural draw near the western side of the house.

Frank went into the house through the back door. He hoped that it was Dan out there, with Dennis and Elaine, the rest of the bunch. He'd be glad to see him. Two days ago, before the storm, Zeb Taggart had come, trying to run off the herd. Frank and his men had stood them off, but only because it had started snowing. Now that it was clearing, Frank knew it was only a matter of time before Zeb made his move. There was no way to warn Dan of the present situation. He was hoping that Dan had seen the campfires and tents out there along the Gallatin and sensed the trouble. He knew that Dan and Taggart were old enemies.

Frank stoked the fire in the kitchen stove and set the stew pot on. It was filled with chopped venison, new potatoes from the Gallatin Valley, onions, and roots, swimming in a thick, seasoned broth. Stew was the only thing Frank could cook well, and he longed for Elaine to arrive so that they could have different fare. He and the boys had finished the little log cabin in the clearing above the spring where Dennis and Elaine would live after they were married proper in Bozeman City, he mused.

John Bozeman had been to see Frank five days before and said the cattle market was wide open, with beef due to sell at a premium. John had promised to notify the preacher that he'd have some customers soon. The other news he had brought was disconcerting, but Frank didn't want to think about that. His main worry now was Zeb Taggart. If he rustled their cattle, they would be wiped out. Memories of beefless winters haunted the mining camps. If they got the B Bar C cattle to Virginia City, they'd make enough to buy even larger herds, to make the ranch grow and show a profit for all concerned. It was a dream that Frank shared with Dan. Now his stomach was in knots, thinking of the men out there, waiting to steal all they had worked for.

Frank's stomach was out of kilter more from inactivity than from worry. He always fretted when he couldn't be doing something. The snow had kept him from doing a lot of things, and he was like a spring knife, ready to snap open its blade. He paced the floor and chewed his fingernails. He looked out the window and checked his pistol. He stirred the stew and ran a hand through his shock of reddish hair. Finally, he dished up a bowl for Lou and took it through the house and out the back.

"Any sign of anything, Lou?" he asked.

"Nary, but the cattle are spooky."

"This infernal waiting!"

Lou began eating the stew. Frank paced and looked up into the hills even though the sun was set and he could see only the bare silhouettes of tree-tops against the darkening sky. This was a lawless land, and Dan had warned him that someone might try to take their cattle away someday. Still, it didn't make the situation any easier to take. The army was no help, even with the new forts. They were supposed to be protecting the settlers coming in on the Bozeman and Bridger roads, but there had been complaints of soldiers stealing stock from some of those passing through. Besides, everyone said the soldiers were afraid of the Sioux. They ignored squabbles among civilians this far up the Bozeman. The mining towns were wide open, and beef was beef. No one paid any attention to brands in this country. It wasn't at all like Texas.

"Keep your eyes peeled, Lou."

Lou handed Frank the bowl. It was clean.

"Want some more?"

"Not now. Later. Get too full, I get sleepy, boss."

"Where's the Wiley kid?"

"Still out with the horses, I reckon. He'll be along."

Frank stomped back into the house to pace some more. It would be pitch dark in a few minutes. He lit an oil lamp and put it near the back door, where it would shine through the cracks in the window boards. He stirred the stew pot again and ignored his own gnawing hunger. He was too keyed up to eat right then.

There was a noise at the front door. Frank jumped up out of his chair and reached for his pistol.

The Wiley kid clumped into the kitchen. He was a thin, homely boy, sandy-haired, hazel-eyed, with bony shoulders and a head too small for their width. He had a crooked smile, made worse by two broken teeth where a horse had kicked him.

"Howdy, Mr. Conroy. I got the horses all fed and put up for the night. Where is everybody?"

"Out watchin', kid. Have some stew, then take some to Hank and Jimmy down at the front gate."

"Is it okay if I eat with them? I mean, I could take all the chuck down there."

"Yeah, go ahead, kid. Just be careful where you walk. The boys are jumpy tonight. Sing out when you go down."

"I wisht I had a gun so's I could hep out."

"Well, maybe we can find an extra one for you around here," Frank said, secretly pleased at the Wiley kid. He wondered if Dan was ever as awkward as this kid. He doubted it. Dan was one of those men who seemed to have been born old. Even though he was younger than Frank, Frank looked up to him. Dan was that kind of man.

The Wiley kid filled a pail with stew, tucked three wooden bowls under his shirt, stuffed wooden spoons into his trouser pocket, and grabbed hardtack from the shelf to carry in his other hand. He wore men's clothes that were too big for him and looked like a destitute urchin to Frank, like a starveling stealing food.

"You really going to look for a gun for me, Mr. Conroy?"

"Sure, kid. When you get back, I'll have something for you to pack around. Can you shoot?"

"I can shoot, but I never owned no gun of no kind. I can shoot pretty fair."

"Hurry down there with that grub, Wiley. Don't be jawin' with Hank and Jimmy all night."

"No, sir. I'll be right back."

Frank watched the gangly kid clump across the wood floor, heard the front door kicked shut.

The minutes ticked by, seeming like hours.

He got up, dug through a box, and found a pistol and holster. He spun the cylinder, checked the barrel. It was a Colt Navy, .36 caliber, made in 1851. He shot two caps on each cylinder to dry them. He got a powder flask and balls, poured the powder in the cylinders, and rammed the balls home. He smeared grease over each ball to prevent flash ignition, then capped each nipple. He put the hammer between two nipples and holstered it. The gun showed signs of rusting, but was otherwise in perfect condition. It would make a fine sidearm for Wiley, Frank thought.

Handling the gun had made him less nervous, but he was still apprehensive. He knew he didn't have enough men to stand off Taggart right now. If Dan arrived with his brother and the hands, they might have a chance. Dan himself might be just the edge they needed to prevent Taggart from taking their cattle. There had been a lot of unexplained deaths in the valley all this year. Some said Taggart was behind them, others said Langly. In any case, there were vigilantes taking care of any threat from Langly. The vigilante group was the nearest thing to law in the mining camps. There were many who held that this kind of law was worse than the crime it was supposed to snuff out. People were afraid of the vigilantes, who dispensed justice swiftly and without recourse.

Frank picked up his own rifle and went to the front porch again. In the distance he could see the campfires of Taggart and his bunch. He walked around back to see if Lou had heard anything more. His nervousness returned.

"Hear anything, Lou?"

"Yunh, boss. Listen!"

Frank strained his ears.

There was something moving out there, up the slope. Moving and then stopping. He tried to pinpoint the direction of the sound. Was it the secret backtrail that only he and Dan knew about? They had chosen this site for the ranch house because of that trail. It offered a chance for escape or approach in case of trouble. Dan had often said that he would use it if ever he had to. Perhaps he had seen the campfires of Taggart and his men. If so, he could well be using that unmarked trail that switched back and forth through gullies that looked impenetrable to the naked eye but were actually coursed by a narrow game trail.

"I hear it," said Frank. "Stay ready, but don't shoot unless I tell you."

He wondered if Taggart could have discovered the trail for himself. His hand gripped his rifle more tightly. The darkness seemed to thicken as he waited, next to Lou.

"There it is again," Lou whispered.

"Shh! I hear it."

The two men waited, rifles ready, as the sound of a horse or other large animal moved closer to them. Whatever it was, it was still high up, in the slope where the last gully topped out. There were no more pauses, however. The horse, if that's what it was, moved down the slope steadily. Frank looked over his shoulder to be sure he and Lou weren't silhouetted by the lantern he had hung. They were some distance from the light cast by its glow and off to one side.

Satisfied, Frank continued to listen. As the sound drew closer, he and Lou crouched and moved into position where they could both shoot if they had to. Whoever it was had to have come through the maze of gullies that separated the slope back of the house from the larger mountain rising beyond them. The slope pitched off into the series of crisscrossing gullies as though some crazed meteor had spun through the land at that spot centuries ago, digging a network of ditches before it burned up or careened off in another direction.

Finally, a horse's head appeared, then the horse itself, its rider. Down the long slope it came, a shadowy apparition moving toward them. Five hundred yards, four hundred, three hundred, two hundred. Frank let the horse come on. At a hundred yards he called out. He knew it wasn't Dan.

"Sing out a name or come no farther!"

"Frank!"

"Elaine!" His voice was choked with emotion. "For the Lord's sake, get on down here. Lou, it's my sister!"

Lou sagged with relief, stood there dumbfounded as the tension of the last several moments drained out of him.

"You're alone!" Frank exclaimed as she rode up. He helped her from the saddle. She was limp, exhausted, in his arms. "Where's Dan and Dennis?"

"Dennis has been killed, Frank. Dan's back there, way back, somewhere. He brought me so far and then rode back. But he'll be here. Soon, I hope."

"Oh, no! I'm sorry, Sis. Dennis dead! I don't understand. But come on in the house. You're weary, little sister, and look half starved. Lou, keep a watch out for Dan. He may be coming in at any time."

"Yes, boss. Howdy, Miss Elaine. Glad you got here safe. I'm sorry about your feller."

"Lou Hardy, Elaine. You remember him."

"Yes. Lou, I'm glad you're here with Frank. Dan knows about the man, Taggart, being out there. I think he went back to see what they were up to."

Frank rushed her into the house, to the kitchen down the hall from the two back bedrooms, where he could look at her in the light. She was a pathetic sight, her skin tight against her facial bones, her mouth drawn and weak, her eyes red-rimmed and swimming in tears. He held her close against him for a long time.

"Tell me everything, Elaine," Frank said softly. "If you feel like it."

"Yes," she said as they both sat down. Frank listened quietly until she was finished. She did not tell him about her mixed feelings toward Dan. This was not the time, and she had not sorted them out yet. The tiredness gripped her now, now that she was under a roof, back with her older brother. It seemed to her that she had ridden a long way without sleep or rest. Much of the ride was not real to her now that she was sitting at a table in a warm room.

A sound startled them. The front door opened.

"I'm back, Mr. Conroy," said the Wiley kid, coming into the kitchen. "Hank says that Taggart's bunch are moving around, like they was gettin' ready for somethin'. Jimmy is pretty worried. Uh, did you get me a gun?"

"Over there, kid. On the sideboard. This is my sister, Elaine. Elaine, this is Wiley. He's our newest hand."

"Gee, a pistol. Thank you, Mr. Conroy. A thirty-

129

six Navy." He held the cap-and-ball pistol up to the light, turned it over in his hand. He spun the cylinder, checked the caps. The Wiley kid beamed as he strapped on the belt and holster. "Pleased ta meetcha, Miss Elaine."

Elaine laughed at the gangly boy putting on the big pistol. Frank laughed too.

"I'm going back down with Jimmy and Hank to help out," said Wiley.

"There's powder and ball in that possibles pouch there. Take them with you. Be careful, Wiley."

"I will, Mr. Conroy."

There was a commotion at the back door. Boots thumped on the hardwood. Wiley stopped in his tracks. Frank rose from his chair. The big man came through the door, his face a grim mask.

"Dan!" Frank exclaimed.

"Frank. Looks like you got trouble. Taggart's getting ready to make his move."

"I've got men out there. Wiley, this is my partner, Dan Brant. Dan, this is Wiley."

"Glad ta meetcha, Mr. Brant."

"Mighty young," said Dan.

"We need every gun we can get. Did you see Gray Wolf?"

"I saw him," said Dan. "No time to explain it all."

"God, Dan, I'm sorry about Dennis. Elaine told me all about it."

Dan looked at Elaine. She looked weary, bedraggled.

Just then the shooting began, the yelling.

"The cattle!" Frank shouted. "Taggart's after the

130

cattle!"

Dan led the way to the front door, Frank and Wiley following. Elaine put her head on the table and her shoulders began to shake with sobs.

Chapter Twelve

Zeb Taggart dispatched his men in phalanxes, like spears, striking in three directions. There were two dozen of them, whooping and hollering as they rammed into the B Bar C herd.

Their six-guns blazed like murderous fireflies, winking first in one place, then in another. The raid was well planned, well executed. In the seeming helter-skelter of confusion, Taggart's men worked the cattle. The shooters rode the fringes of the herd, returning fire from Jimmy and Hank, who were having trouble with their horses. The horses, not used to the continuous noise of gunfire, fought the bits and tried to bolt to safety.

Zeb himself stayed to the rear, watching his lightning attack work to his satisfaction. Beside him was a somber man, Ed Rankin, itching to get into it.

"No, Ed," Taggart said, "my way is best. In the dark you wouldn't be sure which one is Conroy. His gun wouldn't care who you were."

Rankin knew that Taggart was right. In the darkness, shapes against the white of the snow were too similar. It would be difficult to tell friend from foe. Taggart knew where his own men were, Ed did not. Taggart knew where the B Bar C hands were, Rankin did not. From the house, though, came shouts and the orange wink of explosions as someone fired shots into the night. Rankin wondered if Dan Brant was one of those. He'd had time to get to the B Bar C. He'd lost Dan's trail a long time back.

The herd moved according to plan, a thousand head, gathered up in a rush by able men, practiced men. To the rear, picked hands kept up a steady stream of fire while the distance between the herd and the home ranch lengthened.

Jimmy Carter spurred his horse free of bunched cattle that had milled on their position. He had emptied one six-gun, was now snaking free another from the holster slung from his saddle horn. Hank Niles was behind him, caught in the turmoil, cursing the cattle that barred him from getting into action. He had three shots left in the pistol he shook ineffectually as he backed his horse out of the melee.

"They boxed us in for fair," Jimmy panted. "But I'm a-gittin' loose."

"Looks like hep is a-comin'."

Both men saw figures racing on foot toward the Gallatin.

"Won't do 'em no good. Nor us'n either. The boss and them ain't mounted."

"Dammit all!" cursed Hank, finally out in the

open. "Let's go git 'em."

The Wiley kid raced ahead of Dan, Frank, and Lou. In the darkness he couldn't see anything to shoot at. He was yelling, his voice choked with excitement.

"Come back, kid!" Frank warned. "Go get the saddle horses!"

"Aw!" groaned Wiley but he turned back. Three horses were saddled. He dashed back to the corrals to get them, Lou alongside.

"My horse's tuckered, Frank," Dan said. "But I'd like him brought to me."

"See to it, Lou," Frank ordered. Then he said, "Damn, Dan, they're getting away with the herd. I can't see Taggart, can you?"

"He'd be back somewheres, out of the fight, watching." Dan knew that this was the most dangerous of men. Others did his bidding while he moved them around like chess pieces on a board. Still, Taggart would be nearby, making sure the moves were carried out the way he had planned.

Zeb Taggart was watching. And he was very pleased with the way things were going. He still had more moves to make.

A man named Paxton rode up, grizzled, mean, his eyes wide with excitement.

"We're ready, boss," he told Taggart.

"As soon as the last rump is over the river, make your move," Taggart said coldly. "I want no mistakes. Get in, get out."

134

"Don't worry, Zeb. Everything's set."

Ed Rankin looked at Taggart, questioning with his glance as Paxton rode off into the dark, his horse shoeless and silent as an Indian's.

"Another surprise for the B Bar C," Taggart said cryptically. "Let's move up to higher ground so's we can watch, Ed. I think you'll like this next part."

Rankin resisted an urge to shudder. He stuck with Taggart like a jackal follows a killing lion. There was fear mingled with his respect for the heavyset, bull-like man. Zeb Taggart knew how to get men, lesser men, greedier men, to do what he wanted. He was a leader, cruel, merciless, devious.

Ed knew why Taggart wasn't in the fight. It wasn't because he was a coward. It was because he knew his own worth. He was the schemer, the general. There was no fight here. It was mostly noise and diversion, the result of Taggart's careful generalship. If fight came to fight, Taggart would be up front. The cattle were the important thing. This was the only herd anywhere near the gold camps. Men would pay hard gold for beef. Taggart meant to get the beef to the gulches, the miners. He would kill anyone who stood in his way.

Taggart led the way to high ground. He stopped, and Ed Rankin pulled alongside him. He looked in the direction of the B Bar C, the ranch house, lights barely visible through the thin mist churned up by the cattle pounding through the snow on the ground. He waited, wondering what to look for, feeling the presence of Zeb Taggart next to him.

* * *

135

Lou Hardy got Dan's horse, which was still saddled, pistols still hanging from the saddle horn, while Wiley led the other three horses out of the corral where they had been waiting, also saddled. Lou mounted a dun cowpony; Wiley climbed aboard a pinto. Both horses were fat with grain. He led Frank's horse. Lou led Dan's and they jogged out toward the river.

The shots were less frequent, the stabs of flame more scattered. It was almost impossible to see anything, but Lou knew the cattle were being driven across the Gallatin. It would take some time and figuring to get them back now.

Elaine stood at the front door, watching Lou and Wiley ride away. She closed the door and went back to the kitchen, suddenly weary beyond caring. The shots, the noise, the wild cries, all receded into the distance. This was such a hard land, harder than Colorado had been. It was wilder, for one thing, and violence seemed to follow her like a bad memory that couldn't be checked. First, Dennis had been murdered, the cattle stolen. She had been kidnapped, then escaped, only to find more violence with Dan. Now, in what should have been her haven during her grief and fatigue, there was further trouble. Men were probably being killed out there. Her brother was in danger. Dan, too, and that young boy, the Texan. Everything seemed so hopeless. She put her head down on her arms, where they rested on the table. The tiredness rolled up from her feet and she closed her eyes. Her body

136

sagged under the weight of her tiredness, her dark thoughts.

Hank and Jimmy whipped their horses across the open field, finally able to pick targets to shoot at. Their yells carried over the din of the bawling cattle and the gunfire as the two transplanted Texans raced toward the action that had been denied them earlier. A group of riders wheeled from the flank of the herd to meet this new challenge. Six-guns boomed, smoke from the black powder hung in the air, puffs of white. Jimmy saw a flash of flame and reined his horse into a tight turn.

"Over there, Hank, there goes one. Come on!"

Hank twisted his horse in a tight turn to follow Jimmy. They saw two men, then three, with their pistols drawn. Jimmy took aim on the run and fired. A Taggart man tumbled from the saddle, the .44 ball ripping through rib, lung, and snapping the spine. He fell soundlessly to the ground.

"Whooeee! I got me one!" whooped Jimmy.

Another Taggart rider flashed into view, through the smoke, then angled off away from the two B Bar C riders. Hank spotted him and raced after the man, the heady stench of blood in his nostrils. He took aim and was about to squeeze the trigger when he knew something was wrong.

"Look out, Hank!" Jimmy warned.

The Taggart men had split into two bunches and now had the two Texans caught in a gauntlet, a pincer. The decoy brought his horse up short and turned, a rifle in his hand. He stopped and took dead aim on Hank.

Hank squeezed off his shot but knew it was no good. He was too surprised to think straight. He stared death in the face, knew that he had only seconds of life left to him. He bit down hard, steeled himself.

A split second later, a .58-caliber ball caught him just below his breastbone. The air went out of his lungs in a rush. The impact of the high velocity lead ball rapped his rump against the cantle. His head snapped back and he saw the stars spinning like silver firewheels at a whoop-de-do. From his side came another burst of fire and he felt an ax tear into his hip, rip it apart like split cordwood. All of this happened so fast that he had only a short, breathless lifetime to think about it, a lifetime that was richer than anything he had ever felt.

When he hit the ground he was dead

Jimmy Carter lasted a little longer.

He knew he had ridden into the jaws of death. He saw Hank take the first ball and knew that he was next if he didn't get the hell out of there.

Riders loomed out of the smoke and rode up on either side of him. To hesitate or run the gauntlet was to die.

Jimmy picked his target and charged to the left. The man he had sighted on looked surprised when Jimmy rode him down, his pistol held out in front of him, spewing out orange flame and acrid smoke. The ball caught the man just above the nose, slicing upward. The back of the man's head blew away like a pie plate.

Jimmy rode past the falling man, his horse bumping into the other's plunging mount. Knocked off balance, his own horse stumbled, faltered.

"Christ," said Jimmy, tugging vainly at the reins. "Not now, for God's sake. Move, boy!"

But it was too late for Jimmy. He had lost precious seconds. Maybe it wouldn't have made any difference anyway, but his stomach sank when the horse finally regained its footing. He gulped in air, realizing that the next breath might be his last.

That was enough for one of Taggart's men, Perry Lee, who had seen the boldness of Jimmy Carter's maneuver and marveled at it.

Lee was ready. He took advantage of the pause in Carter's flight. He brought up a double-barreled Greener and triggered off both loads of buck. One, two.

The shot caught Carter on his left side at close range. Lead tore through him like wind through the chinks of a cabin. One leg was almost ripped away, hanging by a thread as the blood spewed in a bright red spray. The lower half of his jaw racked into jagged splinters. A temple hit blotted out all sound and sight. Carter slumped over the right side of his horse, his feet caught in his stirrups. His bloody head bounced off his frightened horse's neck as the animal bolted toward the river, gutshot with the same burst of lead that had claimed his master's life.

On the high ground Zeb Taggart puffed up with pride. His men had done well. He was pleased with every one of them, with the exception of Ed Rankin. Rankin had failed him. One of his sons was dead, another wounded. Rankin's clan had killed Dennis Brant instead of Dan. And Ed had lost a valuable hostage, Frank Conroy's kid sister.

Zeb liked Ed, who was as larcenous as he. He liked him because he was older and had a certain primitive wisdom that was often valuable on the frontier. Yet Ed had let him down. Hard. He hadn't said anything to Ed, probably wouldn't, not in so many words. The man was still useful. There were not many men like him, in fact. And who could have known that Dan Brant had a twin brother? He could hardly blame Ed Rankin for making that mistake.

Taggart deeply regretted that Dan Brant was alive. The man was a thorn in his side. Ever since Cherry Creek, Zeb had wanted to kill him. Or have him killed. The latter way was safer since everyone on the frontier now knew of Dan's skill with rifle and pistol. Many men feared him because the word had gotten around, mistakenly, that he was half Sioux or Cheyenne. Not that anyone called him a breed to his face. No one did. That was just what was whispered. Taggart knew better, but he never corrected any of the rumor spreaders. He wanted Dan out of the way. He didn't much care who did it, although it would have given him satisfaction to know that he was, at least in part, responsible for Dan's death.

The dust began to settle, and Taggart saw men mounting horses.

"Now, watch," he said to Ed while drawing his pistol. He aimed it in the air and fired a single shot. "You plan well, and you got no worries."

Curious, Ed looked at the horsemen coming their way. He counted four of them. He wondered why Taggart had called attention to their position by firing a senseless shot into the air. He was about to question him when he saw what Taggart was now pointing at, beyond the riders.

Blossoms of flame bobbed like grotesque fireflies behind the ranch house. They seemed to spring up out of the night, deadly orange flowers on invisible stems. They came from two directions at first, then flew up into the air and fell into the dark hulk of the ranch house.

The flames spread and Ed thought he could hear them crackle even though the distance was great. Soon, though, the night sky was lit up from the flames. The horsemen riding toward them stopped in their tracks and looked back. He could see them stiffen with disbelief. Seconds later they loosed hoarse cries of anger and disbelief and turned their mounts, racing to the source of the flames that were licking up into the blackness, illuminating the roof.

"You set the ranch house afire," Rankin said, stunned.

Zeb Taggart laughed harshly, then spurred his mount toward the river.

"You attack a man from several directions, he doesn't know whether to shit or go blind. Keep 'em busy, that's what I say. They run out of one thing, give 'em another chore to handle." Taggart laughed again.

Ed Rankin followed, numbed by the cruelty of the man who rode ahead of him. Taggart didn't try to hide it. Most men would. There was no mistaking the glee in Zeb's laugh. He was a man who derived pleasure out of stripping a man naked, taking everything he had or held dear, and then skinning him alive. He had gotten the cattle, but now he was burning Conroy and Brant out. It was something Ed might not have thought of. Most men wouldn't have. Maybe Taggart was beginning to think like the Sioux. Maybe the whole bunch of them had gone savage.

He looked back over his shoulder, saw the riders churning through the snow, hell-bent for leather.

Dan, Frank, Lou, and Wiley rode at a gallop for the house.

The slope behind the house was lit with the light of the flames. The horses in the corral whinnied in fear. Cattle, the few that were left around the house, bawled.

The men spurred and lashed their horses, the rustled herd forgotten. Their faces burned with firelight as they came charging up to the hitching posts out front.

"Dan!" Frank exclaimed. "Elaine's in there!"

Chapter Thirteen

"Lou, get the buckets going," Dan ordered. "Frank, come with me. We'll try and get in the back way."

"Elaine!" Frank called. "Elaine!" There was no answer. He ran after Dan, fear twisting his innards.

Dan raced around the corner of the house. Flames had eaten through the roof into the front room. They were pouring out the door, eating away at the wood. He knew it would be impossible to go in that way. There was a chance that the back door wasn't bathed in flames. They might be able to get in and rescue Elaine. He didn't tell Frank his other fear, that Elaine may have run outside to escape the fire and been recaptured by Taggart's men.

The men who had thrown the oiled torches onto the roof had thrown too hard. The back door was closed but the flames had not yet eaten down through the roof. Smoke billowed out of the cracks around the windows and underneath the door. Dan didn't hesitate, but crashed inside. Frank followed right on Brant's heels.

"Get down low, Frank," Dan said, falling to his knees and crawling through the smoke. The men could feel the heat in the hallway that led to the kitchen. It was not yet at a dangerous level, but it felt like they were locked in a smokehouse. They gasped for breath and hunched lower to the floor.

"Elaine!" Frank called, choking on the smoke. "Elaine!"

"Save your air," Dan said huskily as he crawled along the floor. The heat was getting more intense. He could not see except for a few feet ahead next to the floorboards of the house. He kept his head low and tried to breathe the air next to the floor. Still, smoke got into his lungs. He tried to keep himself from coughing. Behind him, Frank was gasping and spluttering.

"Check the bedrooms," Dan said. "I'll go on to the kitchen."

He heard Frank go into one of the back bedrooms. He continued on, slow, keeping his exertion to a minimum. The hallway ended and he knew he was in the kitchen. He crawled ahead and groped for a chair, the table leg, anything to give him his bearings.

"Elaine?"

There was no answer.

He felt a table leg. He tried to wave the smoke away, but it was no use. He crawled around the table, feeling his way, trying to see through the

144

haze. He knocked over a chair. The sound startled him. He could feel the heat of the flames on his back. They were working their way down on the back side of the roof.

"Elaine," he called again, his voice thick with smoke, scratchy. The heat stabbed at his lungs. Every breath seared his throat now. He continued to scramble around the table as clouds of fumes poured into the kitchen. He knew that he was close to confusion. The air next to the floor was becoming fouled, acrid. He scrambled quickly, circling the legs of the table.

His hand touched something yielding, soft. He pulled his hand back, then immediately shoved it forward again.

"Elaine!"

Dan's fingers brushed across one of Elaine's ankles. He touched her boot and traced the way her body lay. She was on her face. He leaned closer to her head, detected faint breathing. A chair lay across her back. He lifted it and shoved it aside, then grasped her shoulders and pulled her underneath him. He had to keep her breathing, he knew, had to get her outside into the clear air. She may have gotten smoke in her lungs, but he was hoping that she had been struck early enough so that the smoke hadn't reached her in any great quantity. Something had hit her hard enough to knock her unconscious, and he did not know how badly she might have been hurt.

Dan lost his bearings. A chunk of the roof fell into the kitchen. Flames licked at his legs. He

145

kicked the debris aside and moved faster, his lungs filling with smoke. He coughed and kept moving, trying to find the opening to the hallway. The crackling sound of the flames filled the room as the fire hungrily ate of the wood, darted downward like ravenous tongues.

He cursed silently.

He struggled on with the unconscious woman, trying to find his way out of the gathering inferno. More pieces of flaming roof fell into the kitchen. He could feel the oxygen being eaten up by the fire, the flames sucking at his own breath. His lungs felt as though they would cave in and wither from the heat.

He found the opening and dragged Elaine through it. She was a limp, dead weight and the air was fouler than before. His breath came in searing gasps. His lungs felt as if they were filling up with sand, hot sand. He took as deep a breath as he dared and held it. Then he stood up and lifted Elaine into his arms. He stumbled through the smoke-filled hallway and crashed through the back door. He expelled the air in his lungs and took another breath.

"Lou! Come on back here!" he yelled, wondering if his voice would carry over the sound of the roaring flames. He laid Elaine down on the ground away from the smoke and heat. Frank was still inside, probably overcome by the smoke. He had to get him out.

Lou and Wiley came running around the house, their faces black with soot, sweat glistening in the light of the fire.

"Take care of Elaine," Dan told the two men. "I've got to go back in. Frank's inside."

"You can't go back, Dan," Lou warned. "Hell, it's an oven in there."

Dan looked at the house. It was true. The front roof had already gone. The back roof was caving in fast. Smoke and flames billowed up out of the bowels of the log house. The heat was intense. He took a huge gulp of air.

"I've got to!" he said, running for the door. Wiley and Lou watched him in amazement, then turned to the unconscious girl.

Dan burst through the door, low. He checked in the bedroom, where he had seen Frank go, staying close to the floor in order to breathe. The wall had burned through. He found Frank crumpled up in a corner. Evidently he had become confused inside the room and had gone the wrong way. He was barely breathing.

A cascade of flame fell from the ceiling showering sparks and cinders all over him. He took Frank's hands and began dragging him toward the door.

A roof beam collapsed, barring his way.

There was nothing to do but lift Frank up over his shoulders and sling him like a deer over his frame. He leapt the burning beam and struggled sideways through the door, his lungs filling with smoke. He ducked, coughing, just as the door collapsed into a sheet of flame. The heat drained his strength. His legs wobbled forward somehow, and he went through the back door, staggering under the weight of the smoke-stricken Frank. He coughed mightily, the air ripping through his raw throat. Fresh air poured into his lungs and he kept moving, away from the volcano behind him.

Frank was alive, in better shape than his sister.

"Pump good air into his lungs," Dan ordered Lou. "Push on his stomach hard as you can. How's Elaine?"

"Not good. She's not breathing good, Dan."

"I'll take a look at her. Wiley, you help Lou. Move Frank's arms up and down to open up his lungs."

Dan went over to Elaine, who was on her back. He turned her over and put his arms under her, pulling up at her waist, trying to force air into her smoke-congested lungs. She was a rag doll, her muscles unresponsive. He turned her over and began pushing on her abdomen. Her face was wet with perspiration. He wiped it off with his hand and continued to pump air into her lungs. Once she moaned, Dan rested.

The ranch house burned to the ground. Frank coughed and spluttered, and came back to consciousness.

"Elaine?" Frank said. He was hoarse when he tried to talk. Dan ordered Lou to take over the efforts to revive Elaine as he went to see about his friend.

"We got her out. Don't say anything, Frank. You gulped down a lot of smoke, but you'll be all right. Elaine's not so good. I think she must have fallen asleep and woke up too late to get out of the house. Can you walk?"

Frank nodded.

"Come on, then. Let's get Elaine up to the cave."

Lou and Dan carried Elaine up the slope and into a provisioned cave that was almost like a small cabin. Frank and Wiley followed. Spruce stood around it and there was a barricade facing downslope that could be used for further protection.

Dan had picked the site of the ranch house partly because of the natural cave. It was like Dan to think ahead, Frank thought, even though he couldn't have foreseen this terrible night. He looked back at the ranch house, a shambles of glowing embers and popping sparks. He felt a heavy weight descend onto his shoulders. At least the barn didn't go, he thought ruefully. The horses had calmed down some, but he knew they had probably kicked their stalls to bits. A horse would not leave a burning stable, and had the barn caught fire, they would have perished. A few cattle milled around the snowy pasture, bawling mournfully. The remains of the cabin pulsed and glowed, occasionally shooting a shower of sparks into the air as a log collapsed.

"Get her comfortable, Lou," Dan said, lighting a candle lantern. "Put her on one of the cots, keep her warm. See if she'll take any water. There's a full barrel over there, where the powder's stored."

The candle threw long shadows on the walls of

the cave. Wiley peered around him, amazed. He hadn't known about the cave, never even suspected it. There were hardwood bunks, stacked, three of them, six beds; powder, ball; cured venison hanging from a thin beam that rested in niches; leatherstocking beans; barrels of goods. It was neat as a pin, and their light was invisible from outside since the large room was offset around a bend in the cave. Wiley walked all around it, shaking his head.

"Boy, ain't this somethin'," he said to no one.

Frank began to breathe more easily. He knelt down by Elaine's side. His sister's face was very pale. Her forehead was drenched in perspiration. She was breathing, but her eyes remained closed. The breathing was shallow, full of ominous rattles. Every so often she would choke and her eyelids would flutter without opening. It would be better, he thought, if she could expel some of the smoke and cinders in her lungs.

"Don't die, Elaine," Frank whispered. "Please don't die."

He held her hand. It was cold, clammy. He could not imagine Elaine dead. His mind refused to accept it, yet the fear that she might die held him in its relentless grip. The world would be a cold, empty place without her. He would never get over it, he knew. Elaine meant so much to him. They had gone through so much together. They were bound by their childhood, their past, and by the present and future as well. No, he could not let her die without a fight. He would not let her die.

"Dan, we've got to save her," he said aloud. His voice quavered, sounded hollow in the spaciousness of the cave.

Dan came and stood beside the bunk. He looked down at the girl. He had never really looked at her before. She had a beauty about her that he had failed to notice. Her features were not as blunt as her brother's; there was a delicacy to her facial bones that spoke of fine china, lace. He wanted to touch her face, to wipe away the perspiration, open her eyes.

A feeling of helplessness suffused him. He clenched his fists, said a silent prayer. He knew there was nothing more he could do for her. She was breathing clean air now, and he hoped that her lungs had not been burned. He did not think they had. There was no sign of hemorrhage, no blueness around her lips or her fingernails. No unusual redness to her complexion.

"Dan? What do you think?" asked Frank. "Is she going to make it?"

"Damned right," said Dan, but the feeling of helplessness remained. She was on her own now. Her own will to live would make the difference. There was nothing any of them could do for her. Elaine had to fight. She had to breathe on her own. She had to. But would she? Looking at her now, Dan could not say for sure. He felt defeated. The loss of the cattle, the death of his brother, and now Elaine, struggling to stay alive—he could not change any of it. He felt battered and licked, crushed by forces bigger than he.

He shrugged off the feeling and moved away. He looked at Lou, then at Wiley, appraising them, working something over in his mind. Behind him, he thought he could hear Frank stifle a sob. Dan cleared his throat.

"How about you, kid, you all right?" Dan's eyes bored into Wiley's.

"Uh, yessir, mister. I guess so."

"Lou?"

"Empty as a hound dog's belly, Dan, rairin' to get after them rustlin' bastids."

Dan walked over to Wiley. He towered above the skinny youth.

"You know how to use that piece of iron on your belt?"

"Yessir, shore do. Pretty well."

"Well, we'll see." Dan turned to his partner. "Frank, I'm lightin' out. You and Lou stay here and take care of Elaine. I'll take the kid with me."

"You're leaving?" Frank asked, his mouth open.

"Got a hunch, if I ride fast enough. Go into Virginia City, get some men, take on Zeb Taggart. I figure he's headin' thataway. He can't make it before I do."

"But you can't just walk off and leave Elaine. She may be dying, Dan."

"There's nothing more I can do. She needs air to breathe and someone to make her sit up when she comes out of her sleep. Feed her some hot soup and plenty of water. Big trouble if she gets too weak."

"Dammit, Dan, you act like you don't give a damn!"

A shadow crossed Dan's face.

"There's something else, Frank," he said, his jaw muscles relaxing. "I held back when we came in because I wanted to check my backtrail. We were followed here. Indians, I think. Gray Elk and a couple others."

Frank let it sink in.

"Gray Elk? Nothing to worry about there, is there? I thought he was your friend."

"Maybe. Indians aren't fussy about such if they think they've been wronged. Stay close to the cave. Keep Elaine inside. I'll get back to you soon as I can. Keep your powder dry and stick tight here till I can bring some men."

"But Elaine . . ." Frank started to protest.

"Can't be helped by me anymore'n she is. She's breathing and that's a good sign. Just make sure her windpipe doesn't close up on her. Breathe into her mouth if you have to." Dan paused, looked at the kid. "Wiley, you want to ride with me?"

"Sure, mister. I'm ready."

Wiley was confused by what was going on around him. He felt the tension among everyone in the cave. There was something positive about Dan Brant. He was the man in charge.

"Lou, I'm counting on you," Dan said.

Lou nodded.

"Frank, my friend, I'm not deserting you. There's nothing I can do here. We've lost our ranch house and our cattle are about to be sold out from under us. Some of the men out there killed my brother. There's some due bills comin up for payment."

Frank looked at his partner. He lowered his eyes sheepishly.

"I understand, Dan. You're right. There's nothing any of us can do for Elaine. And we've got big troubles. I wish I were going with you."

"We'll make out, Frank. You keep a steady hand. So long. Kid, get yourself that rifle over there. It's loaded, just put a cap on it."

In a daze, young Wiley went to the rifle that Dan had pointed out. It was a slender, beautiful thing.

"Lou, give him a pouch of shot and a horn of powder, a capbox."

Lou handed the items to Wiley, who stuffed the shot and caps into his pocket after removing one, and slung the horn over his shoulder. He capped the rifle. It felt just right in his bony hands.

Dan took a shotgun from the arms chest, checked it, capped it. He took along some extra ball for it.

"So long, Dan," Frank said.

"Be seein' ya," Lou drawled.

And then the two were gone.

Outside, Dan cautiously stepped away from the cave entrance. He looked back and saw no light. He was satisfied.

Keeping low, he led the kid down to where the horses were wandering about. He checked his saddlebags quickly and mounted. Wiley climbed aboard his own horse. They rode off, passing the places where Hank and Jimmy had fallen.

"Are they dead?" Wiley asked, his voice choking with fear.

"Yes, kid, they're dead."

"It seemed like they were so full of life. Hard to believe they could just die like that. So quick."

"It's like that sometimes. And sometimes it doesn't make any sense. Or seem to."

"Yeah."

Dan smiled. Wiley was still wet behind the ears, but he had a lot of life in front of him. If he was careful. If some bastard like Taggart didn't come up and blow out his lamp.

They crossed the river and rode hard on the snowswept Bozeman, heading for Virginia City. On the slopes above the smoldering ranch house, three figures sat astride horses.

"We wait," said Gray Elk.

His eyes burned black and fierce.

Chapter Fourteen

Dan and Wiley rode all night. They encountered no other travelers, but they heard elk crossing the road, saw their ghostly shapes in the moonlight. Once, they rode around a blind bend, just to make sure there was nothing unexpected waiting for them in the dark. When the sun came up, they had to pull their hat brims down low to keep from being blinded. The sun made the fresh snow glisten like a sheet strewn with tiny diamonds.

Dan knew he couldn't take on Zeb Taggart by himself. Zeb had too many men, Dan could count on only three or four, and none besides Lou, full-fledged fighting men. He had to beat the outlaw to Virginia City to find the men he needed to help him. He was sure he would find them. Alder Gulch was still swarming with miners. Some 6,000 people were caught up in the boom, many of them broke and idle, waiting for a new strike or a sudden opportunity. Many of the people remembered the hard winter of 1864–65, with snow blocking off the passes, some fifteen feet deep in places, and a shortage of flour. Dan had watched the price go from 27 dollars for a hundred-pound sack to 100 in a few days.

Beef, wheat, and potatoes were the items most needed. Beef was the most crucial food now. There were only a few cattle ranches in the Gallatin Valley, and these were poor in stock. These small ranches were begun from oxen and cows that the immigrants used to pull their wagons westward. Dan was one of the men who had brought herds in from Texas to the Montana Territory. There was still not enough to go around, and beef was up to 25 cents a pound for the better cuts. It could go even higher before the winter was over.

Dan was counting on Taggart bedding the herd down for the night, then driving on into the gulch tomorrow. That's why he was pushing his horse and Wiley's. His plan called for him to strike at night and take the herd into market himself. He knew he was facing impossible odds. He'd have to make quick decisions in Virginia City to get the men he needed. Some of them would not be of the caliber he wanted, but maybe they could provide enough firepower for him to execute his plan.

Dan and Wiley rode into Virginia City late in the evening, but there were still people about. Pflouts's store was open, and all of the hurdy-gurdies were blazing with light. The town was choked with people even at this late hour. The miners worked hard and spent hard in the evenings. The main street was muddy with melted snow.

The town had sprung up in 1863. Some of the people had wanted to name it "Varina" in honor of Mrs. Jefferson Davis. A federal judge had refused to accept this Rebel name and changed it to Virginia City in his court records. Some ten million in gold had been harvested in the area since June 1863, and they even had a newspaper, the *Montana Post,* which kept the gold fever high through its reports and rumors of strikes. Some said Virginia City would soon have 10,000 people and Dan believed it. If the gold held out.

Dan pulled up in front of Pflouts's store. Most of the miners gathered there in the evenings to gossip, to talk of the past, the future, and listen to news from Bannack, the capital. After graining their horses, Dan and Wiley walked inside and the room got still. Paris Pflouts, the owner, eased the tension.

"Howdy, Dan. You bringing in a herd?"

"Paris, gentlemen," Dan said quietly. "My herd is on its way, but Taggart's saving me the drive."

"Rustled?"

"Rustled. They burned the house, shot two men. Jimmy and Hank."

"Be damned," said Virgil Burles. Dave Wallace, another friend, nodded to Dan. Pflouts, Burles, and Wallace had organized the vigilantes and cleared out Pete Langly's gang. Dan knew he'd

158

come to the right place.

"I need ten or a dozen good men with pistols and rifles," Dan told them. "We have to move fast. I'll pay ten dollars in gold to each man who rides with me." It wasn't much, Dan thought. A man could make that in a day of panning, but such work was back-breaking, bone-crunching. Less dangerous, however. He was asking men to risk their lives for a pittance.

"Well, now," said Pflouts, "we could maybe round up some of our vigilantes in the morning. I'm sure they could help out."

"Not in the morning," said Dan. "Now."

Several men turned their faces and coughed. The men around the pot-bellied stove shuffled their feet nervously.

A man stepped out. Then another. Two more drifted up from another corner of the store. Another got up from his chair. All wore pistols strapped to their waists. Dan held his breath, nodded to each man in gratitude.

"We'll ride with ye," said the first. "I be Samuel Dickerson."

"Get your gear, Dickerson. The rest of you." Dan looked them over. Dickerson was a stocky man from Colorado who knew the ways of the West. A good man. Besides him, Bob Anderson, Curt Meyers, Steve Jarboe and his brother Mark, all introduced themselves. Five men in all. "Meet me in front of the store here in three quarters of an hour. Much obliged, Paris, Dave, Virgil."

159

"Good luck, Dan," said Pflouts. "We need the beef."

"You'll get 'em."

The talk rose up behind them as he and Wiley left the store.

"Where're we goin' now, mister?" Wiley asked.

"Call me Dan, kid. You got a first name?"

"Jared. No one ever calls me that, though. Mostly 'kid.' "

"Well, you're growed now. Jared's a man's name. We're going to a saloon or two. You can stay behind or come along. Just don't drink any of the rotgut they pour."

"I don't have no money, anyways," Jared Wiley said, pouting, but glad to go along.

Just then, a man named Russell Sage walked up to the front of the store.

"Howdy, Dan," he said. "You bring the rest of the herd in?"

"Rest of what herd?"

"Why I just bought two hundred head of B Bar C stock less'n an hour ago. Heard there was a thousand more a-comin'."

Dan jumped off the porch and strode up to Sage.

"Who'd you buy 'em from, Russ?"

"Why, your hands, I reckon. Man named Joe, nursin' a bad leg. Said he was gored."

Dan spat an oath.

"Where are they?" His voice was tight, low.

"The cattle? Why, down to the yards. I'm just

goin' to get some money from Paris to pay off. Give it to you easy enough, I reckon."

"Keep it till later. Where're you meeting this Joe?"

"The Silver Queen. He and his hands are over there liquorin' up."

"Russ, don't say anything about this. The cattle aren't for sale. Not that bunch anyway. I'll explain later. I'll sell you a couple hundred head out of my main herd. Keep shut about this until tomorrow night."

"Damn, Dan, are those your cattle or ain't they?"

"They're mine. That was Joe Rankin you talked to. He rustled them. Don't show up at the Queen."

Dan stalked off down the muddy street, Wiley scuttling along behind him. Dan stopped.

"No, kid, you wait here. I got some business."

"A minute ago I was Jared. Now I'm the kid again. Make up your mind, mister!"

Dan looked at the defiant youth. Wiley's eyes flashed. Dan allowed himself a wry smile.

"Come along, then, Jared. Just stay out of my way. I don't want you to get hurt."

Dan went down the street with long strides and turned into the Silver Queen. A honky-tonk piano burbled inside. There was laughter, the clink of glasses.

Cautiously, Dan went up to the batwings. He looked up at the light, letting his eyes grow accus-

161

tomed to the brightness. Then he stepped quickly inside, Wiley following. Dan's right hand hovered near the butt of his pistol as his eyes quickly scanned the saloon.

The room was large with a bar at the far end. A bartender was mixing drinks at one end of the bar, where it was divided by a railing running from side to side. The outer enclosure was packed with men in every variety of garb. Behind the barrier sat the dancing girls, the "hurdy-gurdies," who were dressed in uniforms, some of them. Others dressed more elegantly and probably charged more than a dollar for their attentions. On one side was a raised orchestra platform. The instruments were stacked there during the break. The girls were just waiting inside the barrier for the musicians to come back so they could be summoned with the phrase: "Take up your partners for the next dance."

The din was overwhelming. No one seemed to pay any attention to Dan, who had come in quietly. He moved along the wall toward the edge of the room, searching through the crowd for the sight of Joe Rankin or his man. He circled so that he could come up to the bar from the uncrowded side. He passed through several tables. Gambling was wide open in Virginia City as elsewhere in the territory. He saw games of dice and cards, even faro, but none of the outlawed games such as three-card monte, strap game, thimblerig, patent safe, black and red, or two-card-box faro. The dice game was "legally unfair" in Montana as well, but the Silver Queen was evidently not one to deny its customers some illegality at chance. The dice game, they said, was "fair." Dan knew better. His eyes had learned to pick up the nimble switches from slender hands, the telltale distractions the dealers used so deftly.

Dan knew these things, yet they were still alien to him. He was more adept in reading the signs in the forest, in walking through quiet woods and riding from sunrise to sunset. He had seen both worlds, and civilization was the one he liked least. Yet, he was a civilized man. He had to be in order to survive. The day of the mountain man was over. The trappers and traders had helped to ruin the Indian with their sugared whiskey, and now the trapper was gone, the first to be stamped out under civilization's heel. The trader was still there, buying, bartering, trading, selling whatever goods a man needed. The Indian was next on the extermination list. Yet Dan wanted to keep part of himself free. The ranch represented that freedom to him. He could engage in commerce, but only at intervals. He had learned these ways of civilization as he had learned the ways of the Oglala. He had survived their world. He meant to be a survivor in this one, too, but only on his own terms.

"Stay over here," Dan told Wiley.

"Out of the way?"

"Watch my back. Don't look at the bar or

anywhere else in the room. Just see that nobody gets behind me, Jared."

"I'll do it," Wiley said, his voice filling with pride. He began to glance at the tables, where men drank and played cards, the ones to the far side of the room. The reek of alcohol and smoke was strong. Occasionally, he caught a whiff of perfume, tainted by the other smells. He kept Dan's back in view out of the corner of his eye while he watched the faces of those dealers and players at Brant's back.

Dan reached the bar and took the corner position, took his back to the wall. He kept his hat brim down, but his eyes peered out, searching for the face he knew. The bartender took a long time noticing him, finally came over.

"Whiskey," Dan said, "in a glass."

The bartender reached under the bar.

"Not that tanglefoot. I've got more'n two bits." Dan threw a gold coin on the bar.

The bartender, chewing on the stub of a cigar, his apron stained with dried beer and spilled whiskey, started to say something, but thought better of it when he looked closely at Dan Brant. He brought out a bottle of labeled whiskey, poured it in a thick-walled glass, and left the bottle. He picked up the coin and bit it on the edge.

"Tanglefoot, eh? Not in the Silver Queen," he snorted.

Dan knew the man was lying. Every third business in Virginia City was a saloon. When the supplies of regular whiskey ran low, in barrels or bottles, the proprietors took to making tanglefoot: boiled mountain sage, two plugs of chewing tobacco, one box of cayenne pepper, one gallon of water. The price was twenty-five cents a shot and it burned all the way down.

The bartender rattled coins on the bar in front of Dan, not defiantly, just with enough independence to make the big man suppress a smile. Dan hunched down lower to make himself less conspicuous and continued to survey the room. He noticed the stairs behind the orchestra, and a hallway to the left of that, where men and women disappeared and reappeared at intervals.

Dan tasted the whiskey. His shoulder had begun to heal and he no longer felt stabbing pains in it. Moss and mud and crumbled wet oak leaves had helped it, along with his favoring. The whiskey helped take away some of the weariness of the last several days.

He glanced over at Jared Wiley, who looked like a young hawk, bright-eyed and alert. This time the smile came, breaking slowly, and lasting for only a moment.

"Bartender," Dan called softly. The heavyset man shifted the stump of a cigar in his mouth and waddled over. "Draw me a small bucket of beer."

"You want to ruin good whiskey?"

"It's not for me. Just draw it." There was no trace of a smile on Dan's face.

The bartender set the pail of beer on the

165

counter carefully so as not to slosh the stranger. He took enough change in payment and waddled back to the cash box without a backward glance.

Dan held the bucket up and beckoned to Wiley. The boy came over.

"Here's something for you. Don't look like a damned bodyguard. And don't drink too much of this slop.

"Th-thanks, mister, I mean, Dan."

"Now go back over there and do what you were doing, but don't be so obvious about it."

"Is he here?"

"I don't know. Drink this with your left hand, Jared."

The boy went back to his former position. Dan turned back to watch the patrons. He catalogued every face, every eccentricity of the men and women in the saloon. He hunched lower, kept his hat brim shading the features of his face. He sipped at his whiskey.

He didn't have long to wait.

Joe Rankin came through the hallway opening, a painted hurdy-gurdy gal on his arm. He strolled to the bar and ordered champagne and drinks for the bar. The champagne went for twelve dollars in gold.

Dan felt something burning inside him.

This was the man who had killed his brother, who had dragged him behind a horse until the rocks and sand ground into his flesh. This was the man who had made Dennis suffer like a dog

166

before stringing him up like a common cow thief. Joe Rankin was laughing, pinching the girl's behind, leaning into her breasts with leering eyes.

For just a second Dan could see Dennis swinging in the wind, a rope around his neck. He could see the pain in his dead brother's eyes, the agony in the way his neck was bent. He could see the wounds in his flesh, feel the hurt in his own body. It was a fleeting memory, but vivid, as if he'd walked into a dark room and someone had set off a phosphorous flash.

He stepped away from the bar, strode to the L-joint until he was on a direct line with Joe Rankin. Several men saw him make the move. They watched him quietly with motionless eyes.

Jared Wiley put his pail of beer down and put his hand on the butt of his pistol.

A dealer whirred through a deck of cards, shuffling them. Money clanked at a table. A glass fell from another table, splintering on the sawdust-covered floor.

"Joe Rankin!" Dan shouted above the din. "Step away from that bar!"

A sudden silence gripped the Silver Queen. Joe stepped back to see who had called his name so commandingly.

When he saw Dan Brant, his face went chalk white. His eyes narrowed with a flash of recognition. His lip curled at one side into a mocking sneer.

"Rankin, you killed my brother and stole my

cattle. I call you on both accounts. I come to square them!" Dan shouted.

People scrambled away from the bar, out of the line of fire. A hurdy-gurdy girl screamed, then shut it off quickly.

Joe's hand dipped to his pistol butt.

He was fast. Very fast.

Chapter Fifteen

Men sucked in their breath as Joe Rankin went for his gun. Wiley gasped, froze into a gawking statue. Only one man was watching Dan Brant.

Joe Rankin thought for sure he had Dan beat.

Dan's hand blurred like a striking snake. His palm slammed into his pistol butt and he jerked the .44 free of the holster. The barrel whipped up level with Joe's belt buckle. Dan's finger jerked the trigger once, twice. The six-gun roared and smoke spewed out of the barrel in heavy clouds.

Joe's barrel was clearing the holster when Dan fired his first shot. The barrel was just starting to swing upward to level when Dan triggered the second one.

Dan was faster.

Joe's reflexive shot went spanging into the wood of the bar, low. Dan's first shot jerked him sideways and backward, slamming into his gut just above his belt buckle. The second one caught him high, just under his rib cage, tossing him into the orchestra stand, where he collapsed, bleeding mortally, in a heap of fiddles and banjos.

"Brant! Look out!" Wiley screeched, his voice cracking with excitement and puberty.

Dan wheeled, but he knew he was already too late.

He stared into the twin barrels of the sawed-off scattergun. He brought his own pistol swinging around to face this new threat, but his movement seemed agonizingly slow to him. The range was so short he knew he would be torn in two by the blasts from the short-barreled weapon. Still, he kept bringing his own pistol to bear, and he wondered when the blast from the scattergun would make it all seem futile.

The roar of the six-gun blotted out Dan's thoughts. He saw the man with the scattergun twitch and then his head flew apart. Brains flew out of the side of his skull. A spray of blood fanned out in all directions. The scattergun didn't go off.

"Thanks," Dan whispered, letting out his breath. He backed to the bar and swung his pistol in a semicircle. "Anyone else?"

"The kid done it!" someone said. "I seen it. Took aim and shot him down. Right in the haid!"

That's when Dan turned and saw the smoking pistol in Jared Wiley's hands. He was holding it straight out from his shoulders, the butt resting in one palm, his other hand wrapped around the

170

butt, finger still on the trigger.

"That there was Larry Macabee," said a grizzled old miner to Dan. "He rode in with that other feller."

"These men were cattle thieves," Dan told the spectators. "They also murdered my brother and kidnapped a young woman. Now, I'm needing five or six good men to get back the rest of my cattle. I'll pay ten dollars in gold for every day we're out."

"Mister, you got a gunhand," said one man. "I'd be pleased to ride with a man who can shoot like you."

"I'm Dan Brant. I own the B Bar C in Gallatin. Glad to have you with us, friend."

"Jay Gentry."

"Any more with pistol and rifle?" Dan called out.

A young man with a broom came out of the hallway.

"I'll go," he said.

Several people laughed.

"That's Malcolm Davis, the swamper!"

"You ride, shoot?"

"Sure do, Mr. Brant. This is just my nighttime job. My claim ain't doin' so good."

"Meet us in front of Paris Pflouts's store in five minutes, saddled and ready to go. I need three more men. There'll be a dozen of us against as many of them."

"Who're you ridin' after, Brant?" asked a stocky

man dealing at one of the tables.

"Zeb Taggart."

A current of whispering threaded through the crowd.

The man threw down his eyeshade and shoved the table away from him.

"Then I'm with you, Brant. I'm Bob Letterman."

"Willie Letterman's boy?"

"The same."

"Come along, Dean. I know your pa."

Another man stepped forward. He was slender and looked hungry. He had a two- or three-day beard darkening his chin and cheeks.

"I'm Sid Hawkins," he said, "and I've guns and a horse. You look like a man to ride the river with. I was with the vigilantes. Paris, Virgil, and the others can vouch for me."

"You don't need it, Hawkins. I'll vouch for you myself, though you look lean as a wolf in winter."

"I'm down a few pounds."

"Let's ride, then, if you've a mind to, and chew on some jerky as we go."

Hawkins grinned and followed Dan and the others out of the saloon. The crowd surged around the two dead men as they left.

Dan checked the men he had hired and seemed satisfied. He reloaded his pistol in the street. He bought a few supplies in Pflouts's store and led the pack of men out of town after briefing them on the situation. They had to find the herd, which

172

was likely bedded down, surround it, and wait for his signal to attack.

"One thing," he said. "Taggart is mine, and so is a man named Ed Rankin, father to the boy I killed back there, if he's with them."

It was after midnight when they left the lights of Virginia City and rode out into the darkness of the Bozeman Trail. The sky was overcast, but it was not cold. Dan was grateful for the starless and moonless night. He also figured that Taggart would be too smart to take the cattle boldly down the Bozeman. Instead, he would head directly for Alder Gulch and bed down somewhere in between. Likely he would have the running irons out in the morning. That's why he had to stop him now. Any question of his own ownership could delay selling the cattle, could result in a wrong decision by hungry men in a land where the only law was made of hemp or lead.

Much of the land in the Gallatin Valley had been cleared. Dan was counting on Taggart driving the cattle through the farms there, keeping to the fringes, using the uncleared edges for cover.

He led his men off the Bozeman and across a farm, heading for the line he was sure Taggart would pass. There hadn't been much snow up that way, but the going was rough, still. The horses didn't make much noise, though, and he was grateful. His plan was to travel on the other side of the fringe, keep out of sight, and look for sign in the open where the cattle must surely be driven.

173

He stopped his men after they had crossed into the trees.

"We'll go quiet from here on," he said. "No talking, single file, keep your horses to a walk. I'll be in the open on your left flank. When I spot the herd, I'll join up with you and give you your instructions. Dickerson, you take charge until I get back to you. Jared, you come with me just in case I need to send a message back to the others."

Jared Wiley was glad he was going with Dan Brant. It was so dark and he felt lost among the men he did not know.

"We'll look for light. A fire, a sulphur match. Keep your eyes open," Dan told Jared when they were alone.

The two rode on, looking, listening. To Jared, it seemed like hours. A muledeer jumped across the trail in front of them, making his skin prickle. That was the only break in the monotony of the ride. The country seemed the same, the trees dark, the sky close but invisible. Once, his horse stumbled and he could almost feel Dan's sharp look in his direction. At times he wondered if the other men were still continuing on a parallel course. He couldn't hear them. It felt like they had been cut off from the world, were riding in a tunnel. He strained to pick up sounds from the other riders. He couldn't hear a thing.

Dan could, though. He knew where Dickerson and the others were at all times. His ears were tuned to pick up the least sound. His hearing was acute, developed from the days and nights he spent living and hunting with the Sioux.

Most people listened to silence, didn't know how to listen to the empty spaces between other sounds and no sounds. Dan had learned to tune his ears to different pitches. He could hear soft sounds or loud sounds, depending on how he listened. It was a skill he had acquired and developed. His hearing had stood him in good stead more than once.

He heard the cattle long before he saw them. The sound brought him up short. He stopped, Wiley beside him, and listened for a long time, pinpointing the location of the beeves. As near as he could figure, the cattle were bedded down, or milling, on the William Tysinger farm. He and his brother Ron Tysinger raised potatoes as a main crop. The George Alexander place was east of the Gallatin, 160 acres adjoining the B Bar C. Taggart hadn't moved the cattle far, but he was in a good spot for an easy drive to Virginia City. Bill Tysinger probably didn't know he had a thousand head of cattle digging through the snow to get at his grass.

"Jared, ride over to Dickerson and have him hold the men up," Dan said. "I'm going ahead. Keep quiet as you can."

"Yes, sir," said Wiley, who rode off into the trees.

Dan moved his horse close to the edge of the trees and felt the land rising. He listened to the restless cattle. He would have to get close to see

175

where the drovers were. There was danger in such a maneuver. The cattle might spook and give away his position. Yet it had to be done.

A small light gave him the location of Taggart's camp. Someone had lit a match. It flared for only an instant, but it was enough.

Dan cursed silently to himself.

Taggart had picked a good defensive position. The camp was on a high knoll. The cattle made a sea of horns around it so that Taggart was in the center of a thousand head.

Dan dismounted when he was close to the outer fringe of the herd and tied his horse to a tree. He took the scattergun off the saddle. He would have to go the rest of the way on foot, calming the cattle as he walked through them. He knew, too, that there would be outriders circling the herd, keeping them penned in. How many? Two? Four? More than that?

He waited, listening.

A rider came his way and Dan ducked low, moving into a bunch of standing cattle, hoping his silhouette would blend with theirs. Another rider joined the first, and they rode by, not twenty feet from where he hunched over, gripping the scattergun. A short distance away, the two riders met up with two more. They spoke in low tones, but Dan couldn't hear any of the words. So, there were at least four men guarding this side of the circle. He heard them speak quietly for a few moments, then retrace their paths. There were probably eight men circling the herd, then. These would have to be cut down first. The cattle would probably stampede, but that could be to his advantage. Once they scattered, they would open up lines of fire. If the men he'd hired did their job, the fight should be short and sweet, he thought. His men had the advantage. The night herders were obviously not expecting an attack. They were just keeping the herd quiet for an easy drive into Virginia City in the morning.

All seemed perfect. He knew where Taggart and Rankin were, and he should have no trouble taking down the night riders.

Dan slipped through the herd, working out his plan as he came closer to the hillock where Taggart was camped.

He crawled on his belly the last several feet, taking his time, making no noise. Men turned over in sleep, others fidgeted. He heard no voices.

Pulling himself up the hillock slowly, Dan tried to picture where a guard might be. He looked up but saw nothing. When he came to the crest, he looked out over the top and saw men in blankets, horses hobbled. Two men slept apart from the others. Two men sat on guard, rifles across their knees, on opposite sides of the sleepers.

Dan slithered back down the slope. He had seen what he wanted to see. He made his way back through the herd, waited until the outriders had met and passed by, then slipped back to his horse. His plan was now firmly set in his mind.

177

Dickerson waited with the other men and Jared Wiley. Dan spoke to them in low tones, making sure they understood their roles.

"Jared Wiley and I will slip through the herd on foot from this direction," he said, pointing through an imaginary circle. "Letterman, you and Meyers will go through on foot from this direction. Dickerson, you and Hawkins will take the four men on this side of the herd. Gentry and Davis will take the four men on the other side. We'll give you time enough to ride that way. Those on horses, stay on them. The rest of you will wait until you hear me fire at the top of the knoll, then ride fast through the herd. Make sure of your targets before you shoot. Remember, I want Taggart and Rankin. I'll have them with luck, before any of you start for the knoll. No shots from anyone until you hear ours. Ready, Jared?"

"Ready, Mr. Brant."

"Let's get to it, then."

The men split up into pairs and Dan was satisfied that they understood. He and Jared tied their horses to trees and began the slow stalk through the herd of cattle. Everything depended on timing now. Timing and secrecy. Dan could feel Jared's nervousness, and he put his hand on the boy's shoulder to reassure him. The two came to the knoll. Dan gestured to Jared, indicating that he should crawl a few feet to the right and wait for Dan's signal. Jared nodded and moved away on his course.

Dan crested the knoll and checked his pistols. He had the .44 Remington in his holster, a Colt .36 in his waistband. The scattergun was ready to fire, buckshot in both barrels. The guards would have to go first. After that there would be confusion and he would have to keep his wits about him. He noted the place where he thought Taggart and Rankin were sleeping. A pair of lumpy bedrolls he had seen before, off by themselves, made his guess likely. The bedrolls were no longer lumpy, however.

They were gone.

Dan clenched his teeth, swallowed a curse.

Swiftly, his eyes searched the campsite. There were two men missing. Damn! Where had they gone?

He could wait no longer. His own men would be in position by now. They would be waiting for his signal.

Dan brought the scattergun up slowly. He leveled it at the closest guard.

"Drop your rifle!" he ordered. The guard rose slightly and brought his rifle up, swinging the barrel in Dan's direction.

Dan squeezed off one barrel, and the night exploded with sound. The guard took the load of buck full in the belly and his knees collapsed. Dan swung on the other guard and ticked off the second barrel.

The night herder twitched as shot peppered his flesh. He threw up both hands. His pistol thunked into a snow-flocked puddle of mud. He flew over the cantle of his saddle as his horse, stung by the pellets, bolted out from under him. He broke his neck when he landed.

Then all hell broke loose. Men cursed and rose from their bedrolls. Guns roared and shots whistled through the night like hornets.

Dan carefully kept low, squeezing off shots with the .36 Navy. At close range it was a deadly weapon. Men fell around him. Jared's .36 spoke in the night with bursts of orange flame. The acrid smoke of burnt powder filled the air with its stench. He heard faraway shots and heard the cattle rise up as one great beast and roar with thunder as they raced around in panic.

Dan grabbed one wounded man by the throat.

"Where's Taggart? Tell me now or I'll blow your head off!" He rammed the .36 into the man's mouth. The man gagged. His teeth clinked against the steel barrel.

The man's eyes widened in fear.

"Him and Rankin walked off a while ago. Back toward the river."

Dan kicked the man away from him and stood up. Others of his band were there, mopping up. The cattle were scattered, he knew, but the main bunch of rustlers was broken up. The men he wanted were gone, however, and the job far from finished. He searched the darkness for a sign of Taggart. The river was not far away. Maybe he and Rankin had just gone down there for a drink and a smoke. Taggart, however, was one lucky son of a bitch. He always seemed to be out of harm's way.

But, Dan vowed, he would not get away this time. If he had to hunt him to the ends of the earth, he would. He wanted Ed Rankin too, but Taggart was the bastard who had ordered Rankin to kill Dennis, thinking he was Dan. He didn't need all the hired guns, though.

"Jared, stay here and see that none of these men get away. Dickerson, start getting the cattle herded up as soon as you can. If you tally close to a thousand head, drive 'em into the yards at Virginia City. I'm going after Taggart."

"Take me with you!" pleaded Jared, flushed with success, reloading his pistol.

"No!" said Dan sternly.

He turned to go and a man stood up down the slope.

"You lookin' for me, Dan Brant?"

Standing there was the last man Dan had expected to see at that moment.

It was Zeb Taggart, and he was alone.

Chapter Sixteen

Frank Conroy heard the distant crack of rifle fire. It was so far away, he was not certain that he was hearing right. He stood up, walked to the cave entrance. Elaine lay on one of the beds, but she was not asleep. He had lifted her onto a bunk not long after Dan and the others had left. She had come to about a half hour after that. She had even sat outside on the ledge that afternoon, wrapped in a shawl. She was breathing better now.

He stood at the cave entrance a long time, wondering what the sounds meant. They were so faint, he might have been mistaken, but the sounds were like firecrackers popping under water.

"What is it, Frank?" she asked, her voice husky, weak.

"Nothing. I thought I heard something."

"I heard it too. It sounded like gunshots."

She sat up. She had given herself a sponge bath

hat evening, eaten some stew. Her hair was brushed to a high sheen, glowed in the lamplight.

"I don't hear it anymore," he said.

She got up, walked around the corner, and stood beside the opening, staring out into the darkness. He put his arm around her waist.

"No," she said. "It stopped."

"How do you feel, Sis?"

"Better. A little weak." She smiled wanly.

"Maybe you ought to lie down again."

"No. I'm restless. I keep wondering . . ."

"About what?"

"Dan. I can't get him out of my mind."

"Dan can take care of himself."

"Yes, it's not that. Frank, I think . . . I think I love him." She sucked in a breath as if startled by her own boldness. She had been carrying the burden of her thoughts for two days and a long night. "I know it sounds crazy."

"Are you sure, Elaine? I mean, maybe it's just wishful thinking. Dan looks so much like Dennis. Maybe you just think you love him."

She walked back to the bunk bed, sat on its edge. She rocked slowly, pensive.

Frank stood just inside the cave entrance, watching her.

"That's what I thought at first. No, at first I didn't like him. I thought he was insensitive, rough, crude. All the things Dennis wasn't. But I was wrong. Yesterday, last night, I knew he carried

183

me out of the burning house. I couldn't speak,
was almost unconscious, but I knew it was Dan.
knew when he touched me."

"Elaine . . ."

"No, listen, Frank. I've got to talk it out.
don't dare say anything to Dan. Not yet. It's too
soon after . . . after Dennis's death. Umm, it's so
hard to think about that, and then when I se
Dan or think about him, it's almost as if—"

"Don't say it," said her brother. "You don'
mean it."

"Well, some part of Dennis will always be alive
In my heart, and in his brother. They were identi
cal twins. I can't help looking at Dan and think
ing of Dennis. I know it may sound wrong, bu
it's not really. It's like that young man we knew i
Denver. Remember him?"

Frank stepped into the cavern, sat against th
wall. It was cold by the cave entrance. He fe
more wood into the fire.

"Jamie Lee," he said.

"Yes, when his horse threw him, I thought hov
sad it was. He was so young and he left thos
three little children, and a wife no more'n a gi
herself."

"I remember."

Jamie Lee had been one of the drovers wh
brought supplies to the miners. One day he ha
been racing his horse with some other young me
and his horse had bucked him off. Jamie broke hi

184

neck. He was a very likable young man. Carefree, always smiling.

"Then when we saw his wife and kids afterward, and at the funeral, it just broke my heart. But one of his sons, his youngest, do you remember him?"

"David, wasn't it?"

"Yes, little Davey. Spittin' image of Jamie. Looked just like him. Had his smile. I thought then that some part of Jamie was still alive, would live on long after they put him into the ground. Davey, and Lorna, his daughter, and the oldest boy, Seth. Beautiful children, and all of them either had Jamie's mouth, his eyes, his smile, his nose. Well, with Dan it's even stronger. I see parts of Dennis in him. There's a tenderness there that he does his best to hide. I misunderstood him at first, but I think I know why he's the way he is."

"Why?" The fire crackled with the fresh wood. Sparks shot up in the air, swirled in a spiral, then winked out, one by one.

"Both he and Dennis lived through a family tragedy. Dennis got away, and Dan didn't. He has his own way of looking at things. Maybe, for this country, he's more practical than Dennis was."

"I think you're right there. Dan's at home here. He understands the hardness of the country, the ways of the people. He's a good man and I like him. I just can't see you and Dan as man and wife."

Elaine smiled.

"Oh, I haven't thought that far ahead, Frank. One little step at a time. I just keep thinking about him, missing him. Wanting to talk to him. I hurt inside when I think about him taking me in his arms, kissing me. Oh, I know it sounds brazen of me, but that's the way I feel. That's the way he makes me feel. I want him to hold me and touch me and—"

"Sis, I know," said Frank, suddenly embarrassed. "I guess you must be in love with him. I never heard you talk that way about Dennis when he wasn't around."

Stunned, Elaine looked at her brother, wide-eyed as an owl.

"Why, I hadn't thought of it that way, Frank. But you're right. I loved Dennis. But it was a soft, affectionate love. I didn't feel toward him the way I do about Dan. It's odd, but it makes me wonder if he and I were destined to fall in love. Maybe Dennis wasn't the one I was supposed to marry all along."

"Elaine, you're treading on dangerous ground."

She sighed.

"I know," she said. "I'm afraid. I'm almost afraid of seeing Dan again, afraid that he'll read my thoughts."

"He might." Frank laughed. "He doesn't miss much."

They heard a scraping noise outside the cave. Frank sat up straight. His hand reached for his

186

pistol.

"Lou?" he called.

Lou Hardy had been gone all evening. He should have been back hours earlier from tending to the stock, Frank mused.

"Frank . . ." Elaine looked fearfully toward the cave entrance. Neither of them could see the opening.

They heard a rock fall down the hill, crashing through brush. Then it was silent.

"Lou, is that you out there?"

No answer.

"Frank," Elaine whispered. "You'd better go outside and take a look."

Frank rose to his feet. He kept his hand on the butt of his pistol.

"Lou should have been back hours ago."

"Didn't he say he might sleep in the barn tonight?"

"I don't know. Maybe. Maybe he got too cold. I'll be right back, Sis."

Frank walked around the bend in the cavern to the entrance. Elaine crawled into bed. She slipped a pistol under the coverlet, kept it next to her leg, within easy reach. She pulled the blanket up around her chin. She began to shiver although she was not cold. She looked down at her hands. They were trembling as if she had suddenly become stricken with palsy.

"Hurry, Frank," she whispered.

187

But Frank was gone. He did not hear her.

He stepped out onto the ledge, blinking at the unaccustomed darkness, the murky snowscape below.

"Who's out here?" he asked.

He heard a muffled sound off to his right, a chunk followed by a rattling of gravel. He turned toward the sound and took a step toward the opposite side of the ledge. Behind him he heard a rustle, but before he could turn around he felt the cold steel of a pistol barrel rammed into his spine.

"Don't pull that pistol, Conroy, or I'll air you out with a .44 ball."

"Who are you?"

"Raise them hands, son."

Frank lifted his hands over his head. He felt a sudden loss of weight as the gunman jerked his pistol free of the holster.

"Your sister inside, Conroy?"

"Damn you, what do you want?"

"Move!"

The man pushed Frank and he stumbled.

"Inside that there cave," said the voice. Frank didn't recognize it. He was sure he had never heard it before.

Frank walked sheepishly back inside the cave. Firelight flickered off the walls as they rounded the bend. Elaine lay in bed, the covers pulled up around her neck. Her eyes went wide as she saw the man behind her brother.

"Well, well, well, ain't this cozy as a bug in a mitten," said the man.

"You!" exclaimed Elaine. Her arms were under the covers. She did not move, but stared at the man who held a pistol to Frank's back.

Ed Rankin shoved Frank so hard, he pitched forward, fell headlong to the cavern floor. He turned, looked up at the man who had held him at gunpoint. Rankin's face was grizzled, shadowed with a three-day beard. His lips curled slightly upward, his eyes were steady, like a snake's. There was a savagery to the man that was apparent in the way he stood, legs apart, solid, the pistol an extension of his hand. Frank had no doubt that he was looking into the eyes of a killer.

"What do you want, Ed Rankin?" asked Elaine.

"Nothin' much, girlie. Gonna wait for Brant to show. I got me some business with him. He's a-goin' to pay for murderin' my sons. Fact is, Brant's gonna die for killin' 'em. Same as his brother."

"How did you find this place?" asked Frank.

Ed smiled.

"Did you kill Lou Hardy?" asked Elaine. She felt something boil inside her. Something burned deep in her heart, something fanned the flames of a hatred buried like a coal in the walls of her mind. Her lower lip trembled, quivered with the first stirring of anger.

"Don't know no Lou Hardy," Rankin mocked,

but Elaine knew he was lying.

"You killed him," she said. "He's the only one here who knows about this cave."

"I know about it," said Rankin. "You, Conroy, get over against that wall. Girlie, you just stay right where you are. No harm's gonna come to you if'n you behave."

Again, Elaine knew that he was lying. Frank crawled to the cave wall, propped his back against it. He licked dry lips with a dry tongue. He felt powerless to do anything. His gun was tucked in Rankin's belt. He saw no other weapon within reach. He expected Rankin would shoot him if he made a move toward him.

"Where's Taggart?" she asked boldly.

Rankin laughed.

"I expect he's pretty busy," he said. "No more talk. You got any grub, Conroy?"

"There's some stew. Beef," Frank said.

"Put some up for me," Rankin ordered. "Move slow. You twitch and I'll blow your head off."

"Frank . . ." said Elaine. She looked at her brother with pleading eyes. Frank nodded, crawled to the fire. He rattled a fresh bowl out of a flour sack, found the ladle. He opened the lid to the stew pot by the fire, dipped out chunks of beef, withered potatoes, beans, wild onions in a thick broth. Rankin watched his every move.

Elaine looked at Rankin, then at her brother. Rankin had that same look in his eyes that he'd had the day they hanged Dennis Brant. The cold, glittering eyes of a predator. Memories flooded in on her. She heard herself screaming, pleading with Ed Rankin to spare Dennis's life.

Don't kill him! He's not Dan Brant. Please don't kill him!

She was ashamed of herself now. But not then. Not when they had the rope around Dennis's neck. She remembered Ed checking the knot. She remembered the look on Dennis's face as he looked at her for the last time. Dennis had been humiliated, dragged, beaten, stripped of all dignity and then hanged for no reason. She could still see him twitching as the rope stretched taut, squeezing his neck, stretching it . . . but of course, Dennis had already been dead. Dead when his neck snapped.

Now Rankin was making her brother grovel and crawl. Insulting him. Humiliating him. The same as he had done to Dennis during the last hours of his life. The hatred boiled up in her. She narrowed her eyes and glared at Ed, wanting him to see her fury, wanting him to feel the hatred pouring out of her.

"You bastard," she hissed.

Rankin turned quickly, his eyes widening.

"What did you say?" he snapped.

"You filthy, inhuman bastard," she said. "Frank, don't do another thing this bastard tells you. He's not going to degrade you as he did Dennis."

Frank gasped. He stared at his sister as if she'd

suddenly lost her senses.

"Sis, don't say anything," he said, blurting it out in a panic.

"Who in hell do you think you are, lady?" Rankin snarled.

"I'm a human being," she said quietly. "Like my brother, like Dennis Brant. I won't see you do to Frank what you did to Dennis. You swine."

Horrified, Frank watched Rankin raise his pistol, aim it at Elaine.

"No, don't," he pleaded. "Rankin, don't lose your head."

"Shut up!" Rankin snapped. "Lady, I ought to blow your brains out," he said to Elaine.

"No more killing," Elaine said softly. "No more." She stared right through Rankin as if she were in a trance. Her expression was pensive. There was a faraway look in her eyes, as if she had suddenly come to a decision, as if she had brought her anger and her hatred under control. But there was a deadliness to her calm, a lethal undercurrent running under her placid facade.

Frank felt it. So did Rankin.

Rankin's eyes narrowed. He thumbed back the hammer of his .44, pointed the pistol at Elaine's heart. His lips curved into a waxen sneer.

Frank swallowed hard.

Rankin's finger curled around the trigger of his pistol.

"You bitch," he said.

Elaine touched the pistol lying next to her leg. She squeezed the trigger, cocked the hammer. She pointed the barrel under the covers. The blanket moved, formed a small cone. She stared straight at Rankin, but her mind aimed the pistol.

Rankin saw the coverlet move, saw the blanket rumple. He opened his mouth to say something.

Elaine squeezed the trigger. She felt the stinging blowback as the pistol exploded. The ball tore a hole in the blanket. The hole smoked at the edges as orange flame singed the fabric.

Rankin's mouth formed a surprised *O*. The ball struck him in the center of his chest. The force of the blast shoved him backward. He rocked on his boot heels, struggling to stay on his feet, struggling to draw air into his lungs.

Elaine threw the blanket off and brought the pistol up, holding it with both hands. She took careful aim and cocked it again. She pulled the trigger. She kept cocking the hammer and pulling the trigger, shooting Ed Rankin as he crumpled on rubbery legs as blood spread over his chest and spumed from his mouth.

The explosions blossomed in the cave in a deafening series of rebounding echoes. The noise blotted out all sound, all thought. Rankin went to his knees, then tumbled onto his side. His body quivered in convulsive seizures as the lead balls tore into his flesh. He raised one of his arms as if to ward off any more bullets. The fingers on his gun hand relaxed and the .44 tumbled from his grasp.

Elaine shot until her pistol was empty.

The firelight cast her face in bronze, froze her features into a mask.

Chapter Seventeen

"I'm going to kill you, Taggart. For ordering the killing of me and for the death of my brother."

"I don't have a firearm, Brant. That son of a bitch Rankin double-crossed me. Stole my pistol, my rifle, and my horse. All I've got is my knife. Or are you going to just shoot me down in cold blood?"

Dan considered this. It could be a trick. His own men waited around him. There was no more gunfire.

"Where's Rankin?"

"Got away, Brant. Lit a shuck. Got clean away. I came back."

"Why?"

"Hell, I'm cold, unarmed. We dodged Sioux all yesterday, worked on your damned brands with the running iron today. We had to ride like hell to get here away from the damned Injuns."

"Taggart, drop your gun belt and draw your knife."

"With pleasure," said Taggart. "How fitting that two warriors such as we should meet on the field of honor."

"You wouldn't know what the word 'honor' means," said Brant curtly.

"May the better man win," said Taggart.

"Hurrah for that," said Bob Letterman. The others chorused in with shouts of glee and encouragement. Smacking their lips in satisfaction, the men from Virginia City and their prisoners made a large circle around the two combatants. This was something they all understood and relished. Man-to-man fighting. Fair or foul, it made no difference, they all loved to see a good fight, with fists, pistols, or knives. Knives were best, because such combat offered a challenge as well as danger. A well-honed blade could slice through a man's throat or spear an artery in the wink of an eye. A man could be disemboweled or impaled on an eight-inch blade. Such sport recalled bygone days when men fought duels with sword or pistol, a romantic age when disputes among men were settled with weapons.

"No quarter," yelled one of Taggart's men in a lusty voice.

"Kill him, Brant!" yelled a townsman.

Dawn was just pinking the far hills when Zeb Taggart let his empty gun belt fall to the ground.

196

He drew his large bowie-style knife, sharpened top and bottom.

Dan unbuckled his own belt and handed it to Jared Wiley, along with his spare pistol. He drew his own genuine wide-bladed bowie with double cutting edges and started down the hillock.

"Hold your fire, men," Dan said. "We'll let chance pick the winner of this one."

"Cut his throat, Brant," hollered Mark Jarboe, his voice choked with emotion, raspy as a dried corn husk stirred by a prairie wind.

"Cut his balls off," muttered Sid Hawkins.

Dan stalked forward until he was face-to-face with Zeb Taggart. The two men began circling each other warily, knives held out from their bodies, poised to strike. Taggart lunged and Dan stepped aside deftly, cutting inward with his own blade. He missed, and Taggart recovered quickly, moved back in with surprising agility and speed, lunging, flashing his blade in a swift upward slice. Dan brought his own knife in high, parrying the blow.

For a moment the two men stared at each other at close range. Dan stepped back and stood on the balls of his feet. He began to weave in, stalking the other man. He thrust and thrust again, testing Taggart's ability to withstand his assault.

Men from both sides watched the curious dawn battle. They were silent now, licking their lips, staring with quizzical narrowed eyes. Even those

197

Taggart men who were wounded watched the circling combatants with interest, guardian pistols at their heads. Jared Wiley made a soundless whistle, forcing air through his teeth, and shifted his weight from foot to foot.

The sun rose higher but had not yet appeared over the horizon. The scene lit up like a stage set as more and more light poured into the valley.

To men like Brant and Taggart, knives were natural weapons. Both were as familiar with the blade as with the pistol or rifle. This would be no easy fight for either of them. Dan knew that chance as well as skill would play a part. Both men were careful not to give the other an advantage. Yet, both men were determined to kill. Their faces were taut in the morning light as they circled each other, their jawlines etched hard by granite determination.

Taggart saw an opening and rushed in, slashing with his knife. The tip of the blade nicked Dan's arm, ripping through the sheepskin jacket, drawing blood. He whirled away before Taggart could catch him with the backslash. It was close, though, and Dan knew it.

Again Taggart dashed in, slashing wildly. This time Dan was ready for him. He twisted gracefully out of the way and brought his own knife blade upward. It sank into the soft underflesh of Taggart's arm.

Taggart bellowed in pain.

Blood dripped from the sleeves of both men. Then Taggart kicked out, gambling on surprise. His boot caught Dan in the shin. Taggart whipped his knife in toward Dan's belly.

Dan ignored the pain in his leg and shot his knife hand forward. The two men locked blades, and glared at each other. Dan stepped backward, Taggart following him, off balance. Dan's blade smashed into Taggart's left hand, cutting through flesh and tendons. The wound spurted blood. Dan sidestepped and slashed backward, ripping into Taggart's side. But the blade had not gone deep. It left a shallow, superficial furrow.

Taggart, his face grimacing in pain, turned to face his adversary again, his left hand dripping blood. He was like a wounded bull who knew the end was near but would not give up.

Dan felt a rising respect for the man even though he was responsible, in part, for his brother's death, for the anguish of Elaine Conroy, the burning of his home. Taggart was a man consumed by greed and a lust for vengeance. He should have learned his lesson a long time before, in Denver. He should have stayed well away from Dan Brant. But Dan gave him credit for not being a quitter. He was still a man, and as much a part of this land as the grizzled trapper who had preceded him, the shaggy miner who dug in the hillsides and along the graveled streams. Whatever else he was, Dan thought, Zeb Taggart was his own man, for good or evil, and he would hate to kill him. But kill him he would if his hand stayed strong and his wits held firm.

Both men were panting, waiting. They no longer circled, but stood their ground as if for one last savage lunge at each other. Dan watched Taggart carefully but made no move. It was Taggart's turn. He was offering the first thrust to him—win, lose, or draw.

"One thing you got to know, Brant, before it's finished." Taggart spoke in short, breathy bursts. His chest heaved like a bellows.

"What's that, Taggart?"

"Maybe you been wonderin' how I knew about those cattle."

"Rankin?"

"Before Rankin. Somebody in your own camp. He's on the payroll."

"I don't believe it."

"Makes me no never mind. It's something you got to chew on, though. I never could have known what I knew, though, without this man telling me. I know all about your secret cave, what you planned to do with that two hundred head that Rankin rustled. The man's in for a cut. Rankin's probably waitin' for you right now. With the woman."

"Taggart, you just can't help bein' a son of a bitch, can you?"

"I work at it sometimes."

"Make your move, mister."

Dan set himself, his jawline turning to granite. What Taggart had told him might be just talk, something to take Dan's mind off the fight. Or it could be true. Taggart did seem to know a lot about Dan's business, about the ranch. Somebody had to tell him. One of the Sioux, maybe? No, he doubted it. Maybe there was a traitor in their midst at the B Bar C, after all. If so, he would find out. For now he faced a formidable adversary, a man as deadly as any he'd ever faced.

And Taggart wouldn't back down. It wouldn't end until one or the other of them was on the ground, dead as a stone.

The moments of waiting dwindled to a close. Taggart sprang into action, striking with the speed of a rattlesnake.

Taggart feinted, then raced to Dan's unarmed side. His blade glanced off Dan's wrist and scraped his ribs, drawing blood. Dan, knocked off his feet, stumbled off balance and scrambled to keep from falling. Taggart drove in relentlessly, slashing, tearing at the elusive Brant, his knife like some darting, diving bird of death. His knife ripped great tears in Dan's jacket, drew blood from his thigh, and, once, Taggart's hand grazed Dan's chin, the knife just missing his eye.

The men on the knoll were no longer silent. They cheered and yelled at both men, their words lost in the jumble of hoarse, raspy voices screaming out for the kill.

"Get him, Dan!" Jared Wiley hollered above the rest, his voice climbing to the high registers.

"Come on, Brant!" Bob Letterman yelled.

"Get him, Zeb!" from one of Taggart's men.

Dan knew he was losing the battle. He was hard-pressed to gain an advantage under the savage onslaught. Taggart was like a man with his second wind, like a hurt animal fighting for its life. He seemed to be everywhere at once. The only thing that saved Dan from getting disemboweled was Taggart's blind fury. He wasn't striking with precision. Dan recognized this as a last-ditch attempt to throw him off, and he quickly took advantage of Taggart's carelessness.

Dan held his ground on one of Taggart's rushes, then turned sideways, like a matador caping a bull. He locked Taggart's knife arm under his and shoved his knife into the man's belly, twisting it upward.

The knife point struck bone and a great gasp of air exploded from Taggart's chest. Dan pulled his knife free and stabbed again, burying the blade to the hilt in the man's other side. He pushed harder and felt Taggart's body jerk in a spasm of pain.

Zeb Taggart staggered away from Dan, mortally wounded.

Dan pulled his knife free and released his grip on Taggart's arm. Panting for breath, he watched as Taggart fell to the ground, like some great lumbering beast, his eyes glazing over with the frost of death.

"I—I, uh," Taggart stammered, then died before he could form the word on his lips.

Dan raised his bloody knife in salute, then drove it into the ground, cleansing it of blood as he jerked it back out. He shoved the blade in its scabbard and heaved wearily up the knoll.

"Get the cattle into Virginia City, Dickerson," he said. "Turn these men over to Paris Pflouts to hang. Jared Wiley and I'll ride in ahead of you, set the price. Settle up with everyone and take out your share. There's a ten-dollar bonus for every man here."

A cheer went up from the men he had gathered the night before.

"Thanks," Dan said, and walked down the other side of the knoll. Jared Wiley followed him, holding out his gun belt and pistols.

"That was some fight, Mr. Brant," said Wiley.

Dan, his chest still heaving from the exertion, looked at the kid with stony eyes.

"Taggart was a good fighter."

"You were some better, sir."

"Still, a man's dead. He didn't have to die that way."

"Better'n hanging."

"Yeah, maybe," said Dan, the weariness gathering in his bones, seeping into his flesh. It wasn't over yet. Taggart was dead, but he was only part of it. Ed Rankin was still alive. He must not be allowed to get away. He had a note to pay as well.

"Get our horses, Jared. Let's ride."

"Sure, Dan, sure," said Wiley proudly. His chest swelled as he strode away.

To Dan, it seemed as if Wiley was no longer a kid. He had grown up, maybe.

He hoped the kid would live a long time.

Chapter Eighteen

The two hundred head of cattle loped easily up the ranch house road, smelling feed. Dan Brant flanked one side of them, Jared Wiley the other. For a long time they had been seeing the sun mirrors talking in the hills. To Wiley it meant nothing. To Dan it meant a great deal. On the other side of the Gallatin he had taken his own heliograph out of the saddlebags and done some talking himself. He hoped it had done some good.

He had gotten twenty-five dollars a head for the cattle in Virginia City, the men had been paid off, and Taggart's bunch set to be hanged in a week, those who had still been alive. Now that business was over, except one part of it that remained unfinished. That would come later. He just hoped that Frank and Elaine were all right. Lou too.

Rankin's trail had faded, even though Dan had tried to track him from the Gallatin Valley. Maybe Taggart had been right. Maybe Rankin was waiting for him back at the ranch. He dreaded such a possibility. Rankin was a dangerous man, more violent than Taggart, a hell of a lot more devious. And, no doubt, he was bent on vengeance for the death of his sons. Vengeance was such a shallow, empty feeling after all. Zeb Taggart had proved that to him. The man had nothing left, but he fought on, a man to the very end. At least that was more than Rankin had been. He had deserted his leader when Taggart needed him most. Yet Rankin would die too. Even if Dan didn't find him. Age would get him, or a bullet. Dan didn't care which anymore. He had other concerns on his mind.

He had to find out if what Taggart had told him was true. He had more than enough reason to doubt the truth of what Taggart had said. It might be a difficult thing to prove even if he could find the man who had given Taggart his information.

He looked at Wiley, wondering if he might be the one, the traitor.

Dan shook off the thought. Wiley had come to the ranch after the events that had occurred had been set in motion. No, Wiley was not the one who had given Taggart the information he wanted. Dan could not believe Wiley to be capable of such misdeeds. He showed no signs of selfishness or greed. Nor could Dan believe Wiley could ever betray a friend.

Next to him rode a lad who reminded him of himself when he was younger. Jared Wiley had seen much for his years, but he was as young as the land that spawned him. He could grow and survive if he had the right kind of roots.

Dan looked at the lad and wondered if he could be, if not a father to him, at least a brother. Every boy needed one or the other. Something in Wiley touched Dan Brant and he remembered a time, long ago, when he and Dennis used to pretend they were cowboys, drawing wooden pistols and shooting at Indians, outlaws. It had all seemed so innocent then, but the reality of the make-believe world had come all too soon. Indians had taken his father and mother away. Outlaws had killed his brother. Jared was grown, but it might not be too late to teach him that a gun was just a tool, like any other. It had good uses and bad.

Now was the time to teach Jared such things. Before he became confused and was tempted to take Taggart's path. Jared had already killed a man. It was an honorable use of the gun, but still, such power could corrupt a man, a young man especially. Dan watched Jared Wiley as they rode along. He was a fine lad. He was *hunkashila chistala,* a little boy. He could, Dan thought,

207

become a brother to replace the one he had lost.

"Are we going to run these into the far pasture?" Wiley asked as they passed through the grazing fields.

"No, Jared. Up past where the house used to be. You stop off at the cave and I'll take 'em the rest of the way."

"I don't get it. You gonna run them into the woods back there? You'll never find 'em."

Dan was silent. They passed the charred ruins of the house and pushed the cattle up the back slope. Lou Hardy came out of the cave and waved. Dan waved back. Frank came out, followed by Elaine.

"Ho, there!" Frank yelled.

"Be back in a while, Frank."

"All right, Jared, leave me with the cattle."

"You're the boss, Mr. Brant."

"Tell the others I'll be along directly."

Puzzled, Jared rode over to a spot below the cave and dismounted. The cattle continued up the slope until they disappeared, finally, in the convolutions of gullies, Dan hieing them on until he, too, disappeared.

Gray Wolf and his warriors were waiting for him.

"These cattle are for you, my friend," Dan told the Sioux. "For your people."

"You did not kill Flying Crow." It was a statement.

208

"No, the other white man did. I killed him."

"We did not think you did. We are grateful. Gray Wolf thanks his white brother."

"Taggart is dead," said Dan. "He was the one who wanted my cattle. I seek the father of the man who killed Flying Crow. His name is Rankin."

"We know the man. He is dead."

"Dead?"

"The white woman and her brother buried him when the sun was born."

"Did they kill him?"

"There was shooting in the cave when the stars were shining."

"Thank you, Gray Wolf. This is a good thing to know."

"We will take the cattle. May you live long and grow old in peace."

"Go in peace, brother."

"We go in peace, Brant." Gray Wolf used Dan's white man's name for the first time.

The Indians turned, at a signal from Gray Wolf, and began driving the cattle toward their camp three or four sleeps away.

Dan watched them go, a slight sadness washing over him. Gray Wolf had been a good friend, but their trails would not cross again. He had called him by his name, Brant, not by the name he had been known among the Sioux: Long Blade. Dan sat his horse until Gray Wolf stopped and gave a final wave. Dan waved back, then turned his horse toward home.

There would be building to do, perhaps two houses this time instead of one. Ever since he had carried her unconscious body from the fire, and more so since Virginia City, he hadn't been able to get Elaine Conroy out of his mind. After all, he considered, she must have had some good qualities for his brother to have loved her. In fact, the more he gave it thought, the more convinced he became that she had many good qualities. Besides, a woman was something every ranch needed. And Elaine, he had to admit, was a very beautiful woman.

He wondered what had happened the previous night. There had been a shooting, according to Gray Wolf. But who had killed Ed Rankin? Lou Hardy, most likely. Frank, maybe. Certainly not Elaine. She was a woman, after all. Not a killer.

He rode down the slope and saw her. She was standing by herself, away from the others, waiting for him. As he drew closer, she lifted her hand to wave at him.

Slowly, a bit self-consciously, he lifted his hand and began to wave back.

Beyond, Frank and Lou stood next to Wiley, below the cave entrance, on the flat. A horse whickered in the barn.

Elaine ran the last few yards as Dan approached her. He reined up his horse.

"Gray Wolf said that someone killed Ed Rankin."

"Yes," she said, dipping her eyelashes.

"Lou?"

"No. Lou wasn't there when Rankin put a gun to Frank's back."

"Where was he?"

"Sleeping in the barn, he said."

"So Frank killed Rankin." Dan dismounted and came around the horse to stand by Elaine. "Good for him."

"No," she said. "I killed him."

"You? How?"

"I shot him. He meant to wait for you, kill you when you rode up."

"But you actually shot him. I don't see how."

"I don't want to talk about it, Dan. I'm glad you're back safe. We're all right."

"Yes. Taggart's dead. We got the cattle back."

"I'm right proud of you, Dan."

They walked together, Dan leading the buckskin. Elaine put her arm around Dan's waist. It was bold of her to do that, but he didn't resist. Her arm felt good there. He put his own arm around her waist. It felt right.

It was hard for him to believe that she had shot Ed Rankin. But he believed her. She had a lot of gumption, he'd give her that. He would learn more from Frank, he was sure. Later, when things were calmed down.

211

For now he had something else on his mind. Something that had been worrying him all morning.

Sugarfoot whickered when he saw the other horses. Frank and Lou, followed by Wiley, walked out to meet Dan and Elaine.

"Well, it's over," said Frank warmly. "Wiley said you killed Taggart and that you got our cattle back."

"Sold them for top dollar," said Dan. "Money's in the saddlebags."

He studied Lou's face. The man showed virtually no expression, but shadows flickered in his eyes.

"Rankin's dead," said Frank.

"I know. Gray Wolf told me." He looked at Elaine. She looked down at her feet. "Lou, didn't you hear Rankin come up?"

"Naw, I was in the barn, tendin' to the stock. Maybe I was asleep."

"But you heard the shooting."

"I heard it," said Lou sullenly.

"How did Rankin jump you, Frank?"

"I—we heard a noise outside the cave last night. Heard the gunfire over to Taplinger's before that. From that direction. Later I heard these stones falling. I went outside to check. Rankin was waiting for me. Next thing I knew, he had a gun in my back."

"Is that how it happened, Elaine?" Dan asked.

212

"Yes. Rankin treated Frank badly. Like he did Dennis. I—I just couldn't take it. I shot him."

"Didn't you think it was funny that Rankin knew about the cave?" Dan asked Frank.

"Why, yes, I did wonder how he found us. You can't see the light from the outside."

"Someone had to tell him where it was. Taggart knew about it too."

"Taggart? Why, he's never been here except when he raided us. There's no way he could have known about it."

Dan looked at Lou Hardy. Lou began to squirm. He seemed to have something in his boots or his britches. He couldn't stand still.

"Taggart said we had a man on the inside who told him how many head of cattle we had, where I was going, what I was bringing back. He knew all about those cattle I was driving to give to Gray Wolf."

"I don't get it," said Frank.

"Lou gets it, don't you, Lou?" asked Dan. His voice was flat as a chisel head. "What's the matter? Didn't we pay you enough?"

"I don't know what in hell you're a-talkin' about, Brant. I don't know Taggart. Nor Rankin either."

"Taggart told me you were the one," said Dan, lying.

"Why, that lyin' bastard."

"How much did he pay you, Lou?"

"Brant, let it be," said Lou, his voice dropping into a lower register. "You can't prove nothin'."

"I don't have to prove anything. You can tell your story in Virginia City. If we hurry, maybe you'll hang with the rest of Taggart's bunch."

Lou's face blanched. The blood drained out of his cheekbones. His lips curled back, exposing his teeth. The shadows flickered in his eyes. He shoved Frank to the ground, reached for his pistol. With his other hand he ring-necked Wiley, drew him close.

Dan's hand flew to his own pistol, a blur of speed. He drew the Remington, cocked it as he brought it level. But Wiley's body blocked a clear shot at Hardy.

"You son of a bitch, Brant," spat Lou. "You ain't takin' me to no necktie party. Back off. Throw your damned gun down. I'll take a chunk of Elaine there, too, if you don't get off my ass."

"Easy now," said Dan.

Lou put the muzzle of his pistol against Wiley's temple.

"I'll blow this kid's brains to jelly," threatened Hardy.

"Don't let him do it, Dan," said Elaine. "Let him go."

"Don't you worry about me none," Wiley said to Dan. "I ain't afraid."

Dan took a breath, expelled it through his nostrils. Lou held all the top cards, clear up to the

214

ace. Dan could take a chance, but Lou would pull the trigger, blow off the top of Wiley's head at that range.

"All right, Lou," Dan said wearily, "you win."

Dan threw his pistol on the ground. It landed close to Frank, who was sprawled on his backside where Lou had knocked him.

Wiley struggled in Hardy's grip. He brought his arm up, knocked the pistol away from his temple. Lou loosened his grip around Jared's neck. That was enough for Wiley. He dropped down, bit Hardy in the leg.

Dan held out his hands. Frank leaned forward, snatched up Brant's gun and tossed it to him.

Hardy screeched in pain as Wiley's teeth dug into his shin. He bent over and tried to club the boy with the butt of his pistol. Wiley sidled out of the way, not releasing his bite on Hardy's leg.

"You little sumbitch!" howled Lou.

Dan grabbed the tossed pistol, brought it to bear on Hardy. Hammer back, his finger curled around the trigger.

Elaine dropped to the ground as Hardy clubbed Wiley in the back of the head.

"Drop it, Lou," said Brant, his voice hard, metallic, sharp like the snap of a steel trap.

Hardy looked at Dan, saw the leveled pistol.

He swung his own pistol, up, kicking at Wiley to free his leg from the boy's grip. He teetered off balance.

215

Dan squeezed the trigger.

The .44 Remington roared. Orange flame burst from the muzzle. The ball struck Hardy in the throat. His eyes rolled in their sockets. He rocked back on his heels from the impact, gurgled as blood gushed from the hole in his windpipe.

Hardy went limp as he tried to suck air down his shattered throat. He went down like a sack of meal, his legs giving way as though the muscles had collapsed. He fell in a rumpled heap, blood shooting from his throat in a crimson gush.

Wiley felt the wrench on his teeth as Hardy fell. He opened his mouth, fell backward from the sudden release. Elaine gasped, put a hand over her mouth.

Dan walked over to Hardy and looked down at him. He held the pistol aimed at Lou's head.

"We trusted you, Lou," he said. "You sold us out."

Hardy gurgled. His lips turned blue and his eyes fluttered wildly.

He made a rattling sound in his throat. The sound was like water gurgling down a drainpipe. He let out a sigh and never drew another breath.

"You killed him," said Frank.

"He would have shot every one of us without blinking an eye," said Dan. "I thought he was a good hand. Thought of him as a friend."

"Me too," said Wiley, feeling each of his teeth to see if any were loose. He stood up, dusted himself off. "Boy, I thought he was going to shoot me dead."

Dan slapped Wiley on the shoulder. He turned to see Elaine standing there, shaking. Her hands covered her face. He strode to her side, holstered his pistol, and put his arms around her.

"It's all over," he said.

"Oh, it was so horrible," she said.

"Sorry you had to see it, Elaine."

"No. I—I'll be all right. I thought he was going to murder that boy. And you."

Dan knew that she was in shock.

"We'll get him out of here. You make us some coffee or tea, if you have it."

She looked up at him.

"Dan, is there a place in your heart for me?"

He stepped back blinked.

"Do you care about me?" he asked.

"Yes, very much. I—I think I'm in love with you."

"That's pretty strong."

"I can't help it."

"Well, I been thinking about you too," he said. He grinned.

"That's good enough for me. I—I'll make that tea. Good and strong."

"Yes, make it real strong."

She walked up the slope to the cave. The entrance was shielded by a stand of pine, but the ledge jutted out, a rocky mar amid the green.

Dan helped Frank to his feet.

"Thanks, Frank. You saved the day."

"I did?"

"Yeah, tossing my pistol to me. Lou had me cold."

"I didn't even think about it. Hardly remember it. I saw you hold out your hands and just got the gun and threw it."

"Well, you saved my life," said Wiley. "I'm real glad to be alive, Mr. Conroy."

"Call me Frank, kid."

"If you'll call me Jared."

Wiley grinned.

"I'll call you Jared," said Frank.

Dan took a deep breath, looked at both men. For Jared was a man. A fighting man.

"Let's get to it," said Dan. "We got a mess to clean up."

Jared looked at him and grinned. There was dirt on his face and his hat was crumpled where Hardy had pistol-whipped him. Dan grinned back.

"Jared, we got to get you into town, I reckon."

"What for?"

"Why, check you for the rabies."

"The rabies? I ain't no damned dog."

"No, but you bit a man. That's a sure sign of rabies where I come from."

"No," said Jared, taking Brant seriously.

He looked at Dan's stony face, then at Frank. Frank cracked first. He doubled over in a fit of

218

laughter. Then Dan broke.

The three of them laughed the whole time they were burying Lou Hardy in a snowy gully far from the burned-down ranch house. Their laugher floated on the afternoon air, penetrated the gloomy cave where Elaine steeped the tea over a small fire.

She went outside and stood on the ledge, peering through the trees.

She sighed, content with herself, with life. The fragrance of balsam drifted to her nostrils. A sweet scent, the best she had ever known, and part of it was the air, the aroma of snow on the rich earth, the musk of livestock, all of it. All of it, and all of it belonged to her and to the men in her life.

She looked down at the land and could see apple trees in an orchard, a garden greening out with corn and tomatoes, beans, cucumbers, and peas. She saw a new home for herself and Dan, another for her brother, a bunkhouse for Wiley and the other hands who would come to work for them. She saw cattle in the meadow and goats and hogs in their pens. She heard the crow of a rooster and saw chickens sitting on their nests, laying fresh eggs. She saw the hay in the pasture and smelled its heady aroma, heard the whick-whick of a scythe at harvest time. It was grand to see, to know that this would be her home. Her home and Dan's.

Before she went back inside the cave, Elaine smiled and blew a kiss to Dan Brant.

"The next one," she said aloud, "I'll deliver personally."

ACTION ADVENTURE